OUT IN AMERICA

A Portrait of Gay and Lesbian Life

NEW YORK, NEW YORK

Late-afternoon practice with Team New York Aquatic members. First row: Lillian Forman, Gail Motyka, Lisa Mediodia, John Harbster, Karen Squvigné. Second row: Scott Hirose, Kristin Kramer, Leonard Brown, Tim Baros, David Moniz, Sonja Hubbert, Third row: Johnny Mora, Michael Ing, Bradley Dambacher, Mark Quigley, Michele Huyett, Gene Mignola, Richmond Curtis, Choral Eddie.

PHOTOGRAPH BY C.T. WEMPLE

OUT IN AMERICA

A Portrait of Gay and Lesbian Life

Edited by Michael Goff and the staff of  Magazine

Creative Director : James Conrad

Editorial Director : Patricia G. Horan

Photo Editors : Donna Binder, Jordan Schapps and Amy Steiner

Designer : Thomas Drymon

Project Director : Gerard Santos

VIKING
STUDIO
BOOKS

VIKING STUDIO BOOKS
Published by the Penguin Group
Penguin Books USA Inc., 375 Hudson Street,
New York, New York 10014, U.S.A.
Penguin Books Ltd, 27 Wrights Lane,
London W8 5TZ, England
Penguin Books Australia Ltd, Ringwood,
Victoria, Australia
Penguin Books Canada Ltd, 10 Alcorn Avenue,
Toronto, Ontario, Canada M4V 3B2
Penguin Books (N.Z.) Ltd, 182-190 Wairau Road,
Auckland 10, New Zealand

Penguin Books Ltd, Registered Offices:
Harmondsworth, Middlesex, England

First published in 1994 by Viking Penguin,
a division of Penguin Books USA Inc.

10 9 8 7 6 5 4 3 2 1

LIBRARY OF CONGRESS CATALOGING-IN-PUBLICATION DATA

Out in America : a portrait of gay and lesbian life / edited by
Michael Goff and the staff of Out Magazine.
p. cm.
ISBN 0-670-85850-1 : $34.95
1. Gay men—United States. 2. Lesbians—United Sttates. 3. Coming
out (Sexual orientation—United States. I. Goff, Michael, 1965-
. II. Out (New York, N.Y.)
HQ76.3.U5095 1994
306.9'0664'0973—dc20   94-22341
                                                        CIP
Printed in Japan
Set in Village from the Font Bureau
Designed by James Conrad and Thomas Drymon

This book is dedicated to everyone
who is out in America

OUT
IN AMERICA

Contents

IOWA CITY, IOWA
*Karen Zamora does early morning chores on the 40-acre
cow farm she and her lover, Sharon, own.*
PHOTOGRAPH BY ROBIN MELAVALIN

Out to Ourselves

BY MY MID-FORTIES, I'D FINALLY COME TO UNDERSTAND MY OWN IDENTITY. SOON AFTER THAT LIBERATING AND FRIGHTENING REALIZATION, I ANSWERED A MILITARY INVESTIGATOR'S QUESTION BY SAYING, "I AM A LESBIAN."

by Margarethe Cammermeyer

WE ARRIVED AT the Seattle-Tacoma airport on a brisk morning in September 1991. My father was returning to his home in Maryland. We had booked him on an early flight, so I could drop him off and get to work at the veterans hospital on time.

As we walked through the airline terminal, something at the newsstand caught my eye. On the front page of the newspaper, my face and a headline. It was my first time to experience being identified as "the lesbian colonel." In bold letters. Several months before, I'd lost a military hearing, and the press had been uninterested. This sudden focus was a surprise. I bought two papers. I gave one to my father as he boarded the plane and read the other on my way to work.

My Norwegian heritage had taught me reticence. My upbringing in the 1950s instilled the importance of privacy. And my over twenty years as a nurse and a soldier had rewarded me for obedience. I'd sought validation from outside sources and found it by fitting into other people's expectations. But by my mid-forties, I'd finally come to understand my own identity. Soon after that liberating and frightening realization, I answered a military investigator's question by saying, "I am a lesbian." They were new words for me and had the abrupt feel of a label. I was interrogated, investigated, and offered opportunities to recant. But I would not retract those four words: they brought a wholeness to my life and shattered it. In 1991 my pending discharge—particularly because of my rank as colonel and position as chief nurse of the Washington National Guard—propelled me into a public arena. I had become "news."

The front-page article exposed the military's unjust treatment of gay men and lesbians. That was good. But to have it come out through my name made me feel vulnerable. I had barely begun my own interior journey of coming out when I faced a very public one.

I arrived at the hospital, and looked at the newspaper box outside. There it was again. My face. I froze.

I had never discussed this at work. I did not think many people knew, but now they would. And once they knew, my own homophobia created fears: I would be avoided. My patients would cancel their appointments. The military staff would shun me.

As I stood before the newspaper box, I had a fleeting impulse to put my quarter in and grab all the copies. But that would not stop the publicity.

Instead I slipped into the hospital through the back door and, during my quick sprint to my office, I stopped to check laboratory data.

Then he found me. This old Marine, a fellow Vietnam vet I'd worked with for five years. I was sure he hadn't known. Until this morning. He came right up to me, close, in my face. I had to look at him. His voice was stern, "Do you know," he demanded, "what the most important thing is to an infantryman?"

His weapon, I thought, that's what an infantryman uses to do his work. But he did not wait for my reply. "His buddy!" he said. I held my breath. "And you can be my buddy and share my foxhole any time."

Then he hugged me. And both of us old soldiers cried.

His reaction eclipsed all my expectations and undermined my strategies. I had prepared myself for the hatred. I had prepared myself for the rejection. But I hadn't prepared myself for the love. Recently, addressing a college in Pennsylvania, I departed from my prepared text. I had a new idea I had to convey. The words came quickly.

"What does it mean," I asked the audience, "when someone tells me they don't condone my lifestyle? Does it mean they don't approve of my having a job and paying taxes? Does it mean they don't approve of my going to church? Does it mean they don't approve of my having four sons of whom I am very proud? Or does it really mean that, assuming I am not celibate, they do not approve of what I may or may not do in my own bedroom?"

Though pleased to have finally found the words to expose a hypocrisy, I felt put at risk by my bluntness. I was certainly no longer the woman who wanted to put a quarter in the newspaper box and scoop up all the copies. Yet, as I ended my speech, I steeled myself, waiting for the audience's response. Then it came, powerful and immediate: applause, words of thanks, handshakes, hugs.

Again I remembered that wonderful Marine's lesson. It had come at such a crucial time for me, when I felt alone and exposed. The most important thing we give each other is ourselves—and to be worthy of sharing the foxhole we must be true to who we are.

And prepare ourselves for the love.
July 4, 1994

We're Doing Just Fine

WE WHEN COME OUT, WE WANT TO SEE WHO ELSE IS AT THE PARTY. IT SOUNDS LIKE A GAME, BUT IT'S ESSENTIAL BOTH ON A POLITICAL LEVEL AND IN OUR ABILITY TO PICK UP SOME TIPS ON WHAT TO DO, NOW WE'RE HERE.

by Michael Goff

P ERHAPS THE MOST oft-repeated line in gay and lesbian circles—since the time when our ascent to the front page and the political front burner was a fantasy for a visionary few—is "We are everywhere." It's almost a cliché.

Till recently we've known it without seeing it. Stories fly through our protected circles faster than seems possible, "You know, those two women who live outside of town...they're clearly on our team." "That famous actor...I heard he goes to our church." "The new guy in marketing...he's clearly in the life."

When a single man is profiled (by a magazine which assumes its readers are straight) with no mention of family, chances are he's one of us. The innuendo runs deep: Confirmed bachelor, spinster, creative, musical, strong woman, independent lady, as well as the liberal (and occasionally clever) references to lavender, pansies, male hairdressers, female mechanics, and your mother wearing army boots.

But it's all changed in the past few years—and will continue to change for as long as we can protect the American constitution. More non-heterosexuals have come out, to live as they see fit, than any other time in history. The change wrought by the visionary, brave, early activists means there is no time like the present to make our own decisions about the pursuit of happiness. The AIDS crisis and its attendant epidemic of homophobia has forced the issue and made our dignity a matter of life and death.

Ours has not been an organized social movement orchestrated by powerful or articulate leaders (though we have many). The process has been organic, with little fanfare spurred on by legal improvements, progressive corporations, political challenges, and inspiring role models bravely taking the first step so the rest might have an easier time.

And when we come out, we want to see who else is at the party. It sounds like a game, but it's essential both on a political level and in our ability to pick up some tips on what to do, now we're here. We aren't all alike. In fact the furthest extremes possible are found under the imperfectly named umbrella we call the gay and lesbian community.

Of course, coming out is but the first stage. It is one thing to acknowledge attraction to someone of the same sex. It is quite another to acknowledge our membership in one or more of the thousands of loosely affiliated communities across the world facing discrimination and finding support.

The sheer novelty of our mass exodus from the closet has invited individuals, media, and self-appointed groups to try to define us as homogenous—usually for very worthy reasons. But, unfortunately, it won't work. We are each who we are. Glorious individuals. Which is really what this is all about, being who we are. And we are doing it despite the best efforts of heterosexual institutions that have tried to force us into line for the past few thousand years.

OUT IN AMERICA finds its inspiration in the glorious individual. The drag queen and the suburban couple around a bar-b-que. The lesbian seder and the cosexual skydiving club. It's "reveling in our diversity" and telling everyone (from the government on down) to "get off our backs." How about a bit more *laissez faire*? We're doing just fine.

Bringing it all together has a purpose, since even individuals seemingly photographed at the furthest extremes can learn something from each other. There is wisdom and inspiration to be shared—even between that woman at a high-powered Wall Street law firm and the black drag queen in a small midwestern town. They might not be godparents to each others' children, or vacation together, but like every gay family member in America, they must make decisions on what to take from the established canon—religion, media, traditional family, government—and what new traditions, life choices, and pursuits to forge for themselves. Doing it our way, by conscious choice, makes the lives we live, the work we create, the love we give, and the challenges to society that we offer into a very interesting line of inquiry.

It's why we founded OUT magazine. And, we hope we've been successful at honestly communicating the wonder, excitement, curiosity, and occasional glamour in the lives of the subjects in this book.

Over the last half-century, millions of written words have been estimated, reported and argued that "We are everywhere." This project simplifies and amplifies those efforts, through the age-old law that each photo is worth a thousand words. The sum of the parts is actually much greater than that. Enjoy—and join us—out in America. The grass *is* greener.

Port of Entry

MAYBE ONLY TO AN AFRICAN-AMERICAN WOULD THE PENALTIES FOR HAR-
BORING AN UNWELCOME VISITOR THESE DAYS—MY BOYFRIEND—SEEM AS
IRONICALLY SIMILAR TO THOSE FOR THE HARBORING OF A FUGITIVE SLAVE.

by Eric K. Washington

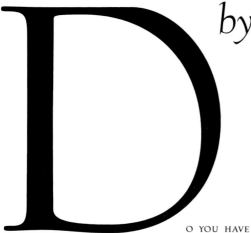

"D O YOU HAVE anything to declare?"

Just my boyfriend, I might have said, but didn't. We pulled over as we were told to, and went inside the station.

Soon the U.S. border official at Rouses Point, his imagination running away with him, was giving my boyfriend the third degree. He rifled through the pages of Marcello's Italian date book, where my friend had been making entries in English that summer, for the practice. "What's this here?" He stopped at 4 luglio 1991, where Marcello had entered: *National holiday*, adding, *I worked in the barn today*. The official read this aloud in a sort of smug, gotcha-you-bastard tone, this simple entry that was going to seal my friend's fate. It did not explain that working in the barn was the kind of chore that a guest assumes—like clearing the table after a meal, or doing the dishes—for hospitality given. "An American could have had that job," said the official. And no sooner had Marcello attempted to clarify that it was no job, but an etiquette, did we both understand that all explanations were lost on this man.

The border official had already begun shaking his head when Marcello implored him: If he couldn't have a tourist extension, at least grant him a transfer permit to Kennedy Airport. After all, he clearly had a return ticket to Italy from there. "That's too bad," the official said, tightening his jaw. "You'll just have to get a flight out of Canada."

Marcello had tried earlier to get an extension. When he called the Immigration and Naturalization Service from Boulder, where he'd been visiting a friend's farm, he had been given to understand that he had to cross the border and re-enter the U.S., in order to be issued an extension. He dutifully grabbed a bus and traveled overnight through Colorado and Texas to the nearest U.S.-Mexico port of entry. He passed right through the gate to the Mexican side without word or greeting, then got on the line behind those awaiting clearance into the U.S. When he reached the desk and asked about getting a six-month extension, the border official just stamped his passport and told him to come back the next week. Confused, frustrated, and now out about $300 in fruitless travel expenses, he returned to Boulder and finally called me.

It took me about 45 minutes to get through the touch-tone menu to a live human voice at the INS. Although she was extremely kind, I explained Marcello's dilemma hypothetically. What my friend must not have understood, she said, was that he had to cross and re-enter the border on the next-to-last day or day of his visa's expiration to get an extension. He could not go to Mexico a week before, as he had done. And what if a person were sick or otherwise incapacitated on the day of his expired visa, I asked. "Oh, that's not good at all," she said. "Then he becomes an illegal alien."

Now it was Marcello's next-to-last legal day in America.

I FedExed him a ticket for a flight to New York from Boulder. I rented a car. We'd drive up to the Canadian border, where we hoped they would just wave him through, like in Mexico, without stamping his passport. Then, coming back to the U.S., we could say we had been tooling around Canada when his American time ran out. But it didn't work. The little one-man port of entry into Canada we'd chosen was regrettably efficient. Marcello's passport got stamped.

And now, trying to get back in at Rouses Point, we were face to face with this border guard who had obviously been watching too much *Murder, She Wrote*. Marcello wasn't going to get any special courtesy for having an American companion, either. In fact, in retrospect, my presence may have been a demerit. "And if you try to transport this guy through another port of entry, buddy," added the official, gunning an index finger at me across the desk, "your rental car will be seized and you'll be arrested."

No need to make a federal case out of it, I also didn't say. The real gun hugging his hip assured me that he and his kind must routinely make a federal case out of these matters. Of course, despite whatever measure of contempt he could aim at me in that moment, we both knew he couldn't block my own continued passage. I was an American. He could only forewarn me that if I got it into my head to try to bring my lover with me it would be a criminal offense.

Maybe only to an African-American would the penalties for harboring an unwelcome visitor these days—my boyfriend, in this case—seem as ironically similar to those for the harboring of a fugitive slave a century ago. It might have been one thing if we were a heterosexual married couple, but not necessarily. We would still be—he white, I black—badly configured, nevertheless. There was nothing to do now but turn around and go back into Canada, to see if we could sort out our mess at the American and Italian consulates in Montreal. But we just sat for a while, before I finally turned the car around, in that median zone between the two borders, the Stars and Stripes in the rearview mirror. Just sat there, like dust idling against an unwelcoming threshold, in that little nowhere strip, denied and, by default, sovereign.

WASHINGTON, D.C.
Miss Liberty attends the 1993 March on Washington.
PHOTOGRAPH BY KIM FISHER

SEATTLE, WASHINGTON
Margarethe Cammermeyer signs autographs at a Gay Pride rally.
PHOTOGRAPH BY JIM LEVITT

BEDFORD, MASSACHUSETTS
Gay Air Force veteran Joseph Smith.
PHOTOGRAPH BY MARILYN HUMPHRIES

SAN FRANCISCO, CALIFORNIA
Drag queens at the 1993 Gay and Lesbian Pride march.
PHOTOGRAPH BY LISA FISHER

ATLANTA, GEORGIA
A kiss at the Lollapalooza music festival.
PHOTOGRAPH BY ADAM TAYLOR

WASHINGTON, D.C.
A couple at the mass wedding held during the 1993
March on Washington.
PHOTOGRAPH BY TOMAS MUSCIONICO

SAN FRANCISCO, CALIFORNIA
*The corner of Market and Castro, the community center
of San Francisco's gay life.*
PHOTOGRAPH BY RICK GERHARTER

WASHINGTON, D.C.
Civil disobedience at a 1987 Supreme Court protest against the Hardwick decision. Over 600 were arrested.
PHOTOGRAPH BY JEB

NEW YORK, NEW YORK
Playwright and AIDS activist Larry Kramer gets a kiss from Molly in Washington Square Park.
PHOTOGRAPH BY ALON REININGER

NEW YORK, NEW YORK
*As the 1969 Stonewall protest grew in importance, its significance
was heralded in many early-'70s protests.*
PHOTOGRAPH BY BETTYE LANE

NEW YORK, NEW YORK
*Family Pride. Grandmother Sarah Montgomery, Morty Manfred, Manfred's mother and father,
and Barbara Love (far right) and her mother on Christopher Street in 1973.*
PHOTOGRAPH BY BETTYE LANE

NEW YORK, NEW YORK

At 1973's Gay Day on Christopher Street, Cynthia, one of the original
Stonewallers, speaks about the lack of recognition given to the transsexual
community for their part in the historic rebellion.

PHOTOGRAPH BY BETTYE LANE

WASHINGTON, D.C.
A salute to gay veterans at Arlington Cemetery during
March on Washington 1993.
PHOTOGRAPH BY DONNA BINDER

End Discrimination!
Civil Rights for Lesbians and Gay Men
HUMAN RIGHTS CAMPAIGN

Lesbians and gay men heckled at a St. Patrick's Day parade.
PHOTOGRAPH BY CHRIS CARTTER

WASHINGTON, D.C.
Wearing the truth at the 1993 March on Washington.
PHOTOGRAPH BY JOHN DiPIPPO

*Highly decorated Eagle Scout James Dale, who was expelled
from his position as assistant Scoutmaster when the Boy
Scouts of America learned he was gay.*

PHOTOGRAPH BY MARC GELLER

WASHINGTON, D.C.

At a Gay and Lesbian March on Washington.

PHOTOGRAPH BY DONNA BINDER

CAMBRIDGE, MASSACHUSETTS
*Openly gay photography instructor Al Ferreira at Cambridge Rindge
and Latin School in class with lesbian student Jessica Byers. Ferriera is the
director of Project 10 East, a gay and lesbian youth support project.*
PHOTOGRAPH BY MARILYN HUMPHRIES

North to the Future

THERE'S THIS WHOLE FEAR THAT THERE'S SOME UNDERLYING DARK, SCARY
CLOUD OUT THERE THAT WILL ATTACK YOU IF YOU'RE PUBLICLY OUT. FOR A
LOT OF PEOPLE I WAS THE FIRST OPENLY GAY OR LESBIAN PERSON THEY KNEW.

by Robin Stevens

THERE HASN'T
been a Gay Pride march in Alaska since before
Kim Severson moved there. She heard about it
shortly after she relocated from Seattle to take
a job as metro reporter at the *Anchorage Daily
News.* "It consisted of eight people walking
down Main Street with paper bags on their
heads," says Kim, who admits it was a culture
shock to leave Seattle, where it was "easy" to
be out.

"There's this whole fear here that there's
some underlying dark, scary cloud out there
that will attack you if you're publicly out," she
says. On the job at the *Daily News* Kim found
that "For a lot of people I was the first openly
gay or lesbian person they knew." Her girlfriend had moved to Alaska with her (the
paper had financially assisted both in their
move), and suddenly she found that she felt "a

lot of pressure to show this face, like, 'See we're
just like you, me and my spouse here.'"
Socially, Kim found her "gay radar" way off. "It
doesn't work up here," she laughs. "When I
first moved, I'd see women doing hard work—
looking all independent, strong, and lesbian-
like. Then they'd hop in a car with their hus-
bands and drive off to mush dogs or home-
stead. That really screwed me up for a while."

Although she didn't intend to be "the gay
reporter" at the paper, when she arrived Kim
found that no one had written about the lesbian
or gay community. "The very fact that there are
gay people in our community makes news. I
spent a lot of my first couple of years doing
those kinds of stories, because they just hadn't
been done."

And as she wrote, Kim discovered the
unspoken rules of lesbian and gay life outside of
"the lower 48." The long nights—at the height of
winter the sun rises at 10 A.M. and sets by 3:30
P.M.—can make people feel isolated and vulnerable. Most of the lesbians and gay men she met
feel a lot safer in the closet, and they're reluc-
tant to talk to a reporter. "The longer I'm up
here, the less tolerance I have for people who
aren't out," Kim admits. "I appreciate that it's
risky, and I appreciate that everybody does not
work in a place like I do, but, man, until we

get rid of the fear in ourselves, how can we
expect others not to feel fearful?"

While Kim maintains a traditional journalist's distance from any sort of political activity,
Anchorage is a small city, and at times she's
found that her reputation has preceded her.
When reporting on the Christian Right—which
maintains a small but significant presence in the
city—she's had sources refer to her sexual
orientation, or to the *News* as "that paper that
hires queers," and admits to feeling vulnerable at
times. "Sometimes it's scary to be out and gay,
because it doesn't feel like there are enough
people here. It doesn't seem like there are
enough people to stand up for me."

Alaska is three times the size of Texas, but
there are only 600,000 people in the state, and
250,000 of them are in Anchorage. An annual
lesbian and gay community picnic draws 200
people in a good year. Although at times it's
been difficult to be one of the only openly gay
people she knows—she's since been joined at
the paper by an openly gay man—"It's been
really good for me to live here. It's settled
some of my convictions and made me walk
my talk a little more. It's really easy to be all
for being out and open when it's easy. When
it's hard, it's like, 'Oh...I've got to actually do
the work now.'"

MINNEAPOLIS, MINNESOTA
An afternoon on the job for glass artist Daniel Tousignant.
PHOTOGRAPH BY KEL KELLER

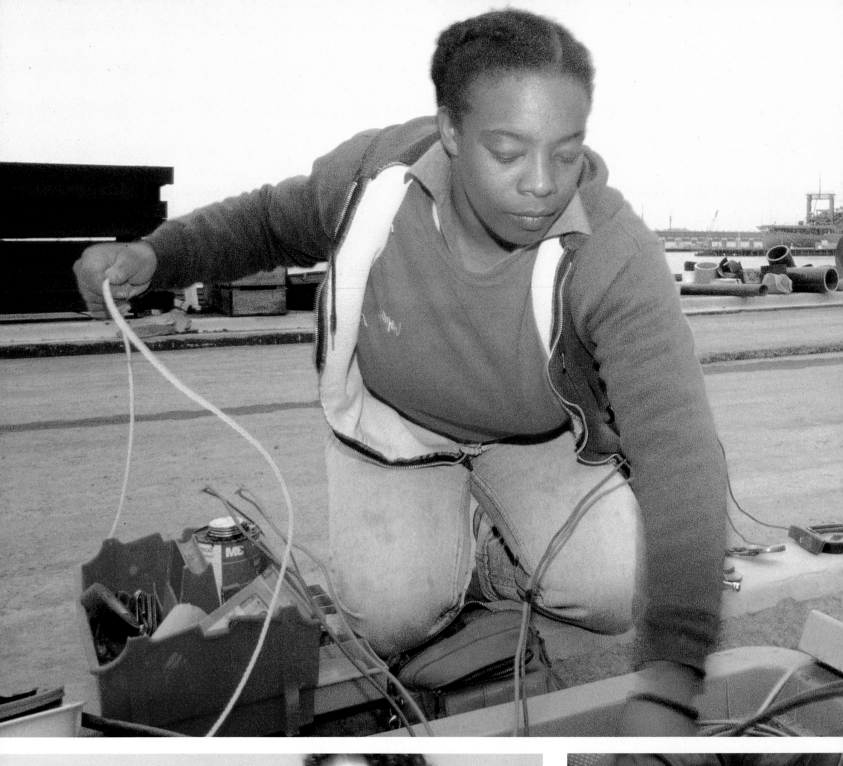

SAN FRANCISCO, CALIFORNIA
Terry Lethridge, freelance electrician, on-site at the Port of Oakland.
PHOTOGRAPH BY JILL POSENER

NEW YORK, NEW YORK
Fashion designer Isaac Mizrahi prepares backstage before showing his fall 1992 menswear collection.
PHOTOGRAPHS BY HAIM ARIAV

CHICAGO, ILLINOIS
Kim Pierce, co-owner of the Outspok'n Bike Shop.
PHOTOGRAPH BY PETER ROSS

MILWAUKEE, WISCONSIN
Research scientist Michael Hayward preparing lab tests.
PHOTOGRAPH BY PETER ROSS

LITTLE ROCK, ARKANSAS

Shana Saunders and Eric Camp send out a positive message
with their gay and lesbian radio show on KABS.

PHOTOGRAPH BY DIXIE KNIGHT

NORTHAMPTON, MASSACHUSETTS
*The staff of the all-lesbian WOW Productions planning
their annual women's festival.*
PHOTOGRAPH BY NAJLAH FEANNY

CAMBRIDGE, MASSACHUSETTS
Boomer Kennedy, owner of Chicago Auto.
PHOTOGRAPH BY MARILYN HUMPHRIES

LINCOLN, NEBRASKA
Pat's Shoe Repair, Pat at work.
PHOTOGRAPH BY ROBIN TRIMARCHI

CLEVELAND, OHIO
Anna Marie Redichi, a member of Hard-Hatted Women,
on the job for a major crane manufacturer.
PHOTOGRAPH BY JEB

MIAMI, FLORIDA
*Jody McDonald preparing contestants for a South
Beach beauty pageant.*
PHOTOGRAPH BY ALEXIS RODRIGUEZ-DUARTE

CHICAGO, ILLINOIS
*Lakeview antique dealer Dennis Daurer shows J.W. Schwartz
one of the American collectibles in his shop, Millennium.*
PHOTOGRAPH BY GERARD SANTOS

WASHINGTON, D.C.
Tim McCarthy, of the Gay Cable Network, the first official
White House reporter to represent the gay press.
PHOTOGRAPH BY CLAUDIO VAZQUEZ

BOSTON, MASSACHUSETTS
Officer Norman Hill Jr., the Boston Police Department's
liaison to the gay and lesbian community.
PHOTOGRAPH BY TOM MCKITTERICK

MIAMI, FLORIDA
*Guillermo Gonzalez, Cuban jewelry designer, crafts
a necklace at home in South Beach.*
PHOTOGRAPH BY ALEXIS RODRIGUEZ-DUARTE

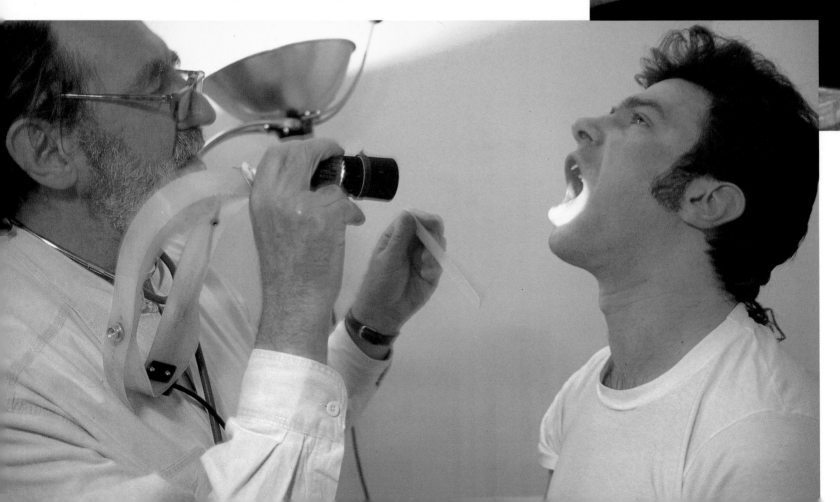

NEW YORK, NEW YORK
Joseph Sonnabend examines HIV-positive
patient Edward Kortis at his office.
PHOTOGRAPH BY TOM MCKITTERICK

GRAND RAPIDS, MICHIGAN
Susie Gay Keillor in the kitchen of the Ramblin'
Inn, a lesbian-owned diner.
PHOTOGRAPH BY JEB

NEW YORK, NEW YORK
Author Edmund White at a friend's home.
PHOTOGRAPH BY C.T. WEMPLE

NEW YORK, NEW YORK
New York Philharmonic member Sarah Bullen at the
Manhattan School of Music, where she teaches.
PHOTOGRAPH BY GREG WEINER

MISSOULA, MONTANA
Kelly at the Catalyst, her coffee shop.
PHOTOGRAPH BY KURT WILSON

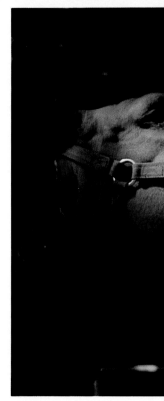

HONOLULU, HAWAII
*Dr. Rebecca Rhoades of the Hawaiian
Humane Society asks a patient to open wide.*
PHOTOGRAPH BY TANIA JO INGRAHM

SAN FRANCISCO, CALIFORNIA
*Naomi Torres, supervisory Park Ranger of the National Park
Service. She is guiding visitors around Alcatraz Island.*
PHOTOGRAPH BY RICK GERHARTER

OMAHA, NEBRASKA
Dick Brown settles a customer in at his salon, BJ's.
PHOTOGRAPH BY ROBIN TRIMARCHI

Movie for the Bluest Night

PEOPLE ARE CRYING. THE WOMAN BACK THERE WHO SAID "FAGGOTS" IS SILENT. THE WOMAN NEXT TO ME WIPES HER EYES. I COULD STAND AND CHEER. A TINY REVOLUTION HAS TAKEN PLACE HERE. IT WILL HAPPEN AGAIN, LATER TONIGHT.

by Jess Cagle

SUNDAY—A WORK night, a school night—the bluest night of the week. And it is raining outside. But here in the dark, the clouds over the crowd clear and a few of us join in song:

Thank you for coming to Loew's. Sit back and relax. Enjoy the show.

Nearly a sellout. Mostly straight. Well, of course. Look at the title: *Four Weddings and a Funeral.* Many heterosexuals I know like weddings. Can't blame them. If there were an institutionalized ceremony celebrating homosexual mating rituals, I'd go. Imagine. Instead of throwing rice, the fertility symbol, we could toss pennies, for disposable income. And our dresses would be better. The movie begins with Elton John singing "They're Writing Songs of Love (But Not for Me)," and his voice sounds deeper and richer than usual. Enter Hugh Grant.

"Strapping buck," says the man next to me. I'm not alone.

The story: Fetching Hugh meets the equally fetching, if marginally talented, Andie MacDowell at Wedding Number One. Flirting. Sex. Complications. Three more weddings. Emoting in the rain. Happy ending. There is a gay couple among Hugh's friends, Matthew and

Gareth. All movies must have a gay character now, as surely as Lucy and Ricky had to keep one foot on the floor. A chic lesbian will do, but a kindly gay male neighbor stroking a cat will do better. I sweat when these characters show up on the screen—George Carlin as the lonely, flower-toting faggot in *The Prince of Tides*, Harvey Fierstein as Uncle Tom in *Mrs. Doubtfire.*

I'm sweating now. Matthew wipes some schmutz from Gareth's unwieldy beard. Matthew watches Gareth cut a rug and recalls to a friend the first time he saw Gareth on a dance floor. Clearly, these men are more than friends. The woman behind me, a talker, wonders aloud—very aloud—to her friend, "Are they faggots?"

But boisterous Gareth wins her over. He gets the best lines. He theorizes that the marriage proposal always occurs during a lapse in conversation, calls it "the definitive ice breaker." "It's Brigadoon!" he declares when faced with a room full of dancing Scotsmen in their kilts. He toasts, with his dear friends, "True love, in whatever shape or form it may come." I have stopped sweating, without realizing it.

It is Gareth's funeral to which the title refers. The church is simple, in contrast to the three florid weddings preceding it. A factory belches smoke into the gray sky not far from where he's laid to rest. Matthew reads from Auden, whom he calls "another splendid bugger."

He was my North, my South, my East and West/ My working week and my Sunday rest,/ My noon, my midnight, my talk, my song;/ I thought that love would last forever:/ I was wrong.

People are crying. The woman back there who said "faggots" is silent. The woman next to me wipes her eyes. I could stand and cheer.

A tiny revolution has taken place here. It will happen again, later tonight, when another audience files into this theater. And it will happen tomorrow afternoon, as matinees unreel across the country. The three hundred or so people staring at this screen have accepted Gareth and Matthew. What's more—and this is astonishing—they have accepted Gareth's and Matthew's love for each other. Not even *Philadelphia*, itself an estimable effort, asked the audience to go that far.

The gay lovers are woven seamlessly into the film's tapestry. No gold thread, no fringe setting them off, announcing their presence. Likewise, here I sit, drying my eyes, a seamless part of this audience now. I can hear the voices spilling out those bungalow windows on the Paramount Studios lot, and echoing down hallways over at Disney during the next few months. "What do we do with our gay character?" someone will say during a story meeting. Maybe someone will mention *Four Weddings and a Funeral*. And maybe, before long, the question won't be asked at all.

People laugh at Andie MacDowell near the end. "She can't act," someone says loudly. Hoots of agreement. More laughter. Everyone's a critic. In this case, everyone's right. The film's sinfully satisfying closing montage announces the fate of the characters by way of wedding photos. One woman finds her mate in a big strapping Texan, another with Prince Charles. The merry widow Matthew appears, pouring champagne with a new lover, celebrating, smiling. Playing behind me, there is sweet, happy music. This is from the woman who said "faggots" not ninety minutes ago:

"Oh, he found someone, too."

BALTIMORE, MARYLAND
Director John Waters on the set of Serial Mom.
PHOTOGRAPH BY PHILLIP CARUSO

NEW YORK, NEW YORK
Go Fish *director, co-writer, and co-producer
Rose Troche.*
PHOTOGRAPH BY KLAUS SCHONWIESE

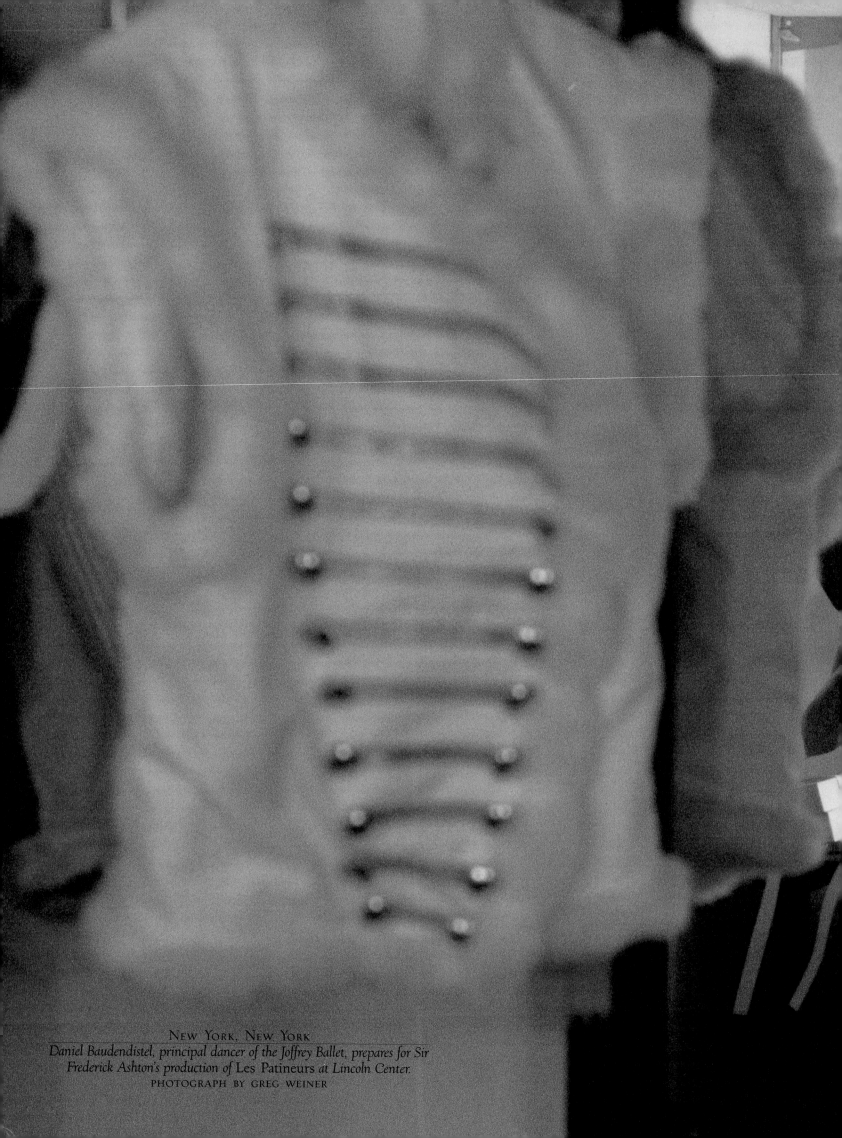

NEW YORK, NEW YORK
Daniel Baudendistel, principal dancer of the Joffrey Ballet, prepares for Sir Frederick Ashton's production of Les Patineurs *at Lincoln Center.*
PHOTOGRAPH BY GREG WEINER

PROVINCETOWN, MASSACHUSETTS
Comedian Kate Clinton at home.
PHOTOGRAPH BY PASCALE DE LAUBIER

SAN FRANCISCO, CALIFORNIA
*Roddy Bottum, keyboardist of the heavy metal
band Faith No More.*
PHOTOGRAPH BY PHYLLIS CHRISTOPHER

SAN FRANCISCO, CALIFORNIA
Andy Bell, of pop group Erasure, performs at the Orpheum Theater.
PHOTOGRAPH BY MARC GELLER

SAN FRANCISCO, CALIFORNIA
Director Gus Van Sant edits Even Cowgirls
Get the Blues.
PHOTOGRAPH BY MARC GELLER

BOSTON, MASSACHUSETTS
Dancer Bill T. Jones in tech rehearsal.
PHOTOGRAPH BY TOM MCKITTERICK

NEW YORK, NEW YORK
Boy George at Industria Superstudios during a 1993
photo shoot for US magazine.
PHOTOGRAPH BY MARY ELLEN MARK

New York, New York
Comedian Lea Delaria and her lip schtick.
PHOTOGRAPH BY LIMOR INBAR

MINNEAPOLIS, MINNESOTA
Charles N. Blake III, Mandan Sisseston Sioux, in the lead role of Black
Elk Speaks. Blake is also the co-founder of the American Indian
Theater Project in Minneapolis.
PHOTOGRAPH BY KEL KELLER

SAN FRANCISCO, CALIFORNIA
*Grip Michael Prince cleans up during Falcon Studio's
production of Billy's Tale.*
PHOTOGRAPH BY KEN PROBST

PHILADELPHIA, PENNSYLVANIA
*Camille Paglia gets an "onscreen" kiss from
lover Allison Maddox.*
PHOTOGRAPH BY ERICA FREUDENSTEIN

New York, New York
RuPaul at Wigstock in Tompkins Square Park, 1993.
PHOTOGRAPH BY BRIAN PALMER

AUSTIN, TEXAS
Powersnatch revs it up live for Austin Community Television, with Darcy Doublas on bass and Terri Lord on drums.
PHOTOGRAPH BY LISA A. DAVIS

SAN FRANCISCO, CALIFORNIA
Pomo Afro Homos *on Comedy Central's* Out
There *special,* 1993.
PHOTOGRAPH BY PHYLLIS CHRISTOPHER

SAN FRANCISCO, CALIFORNIA
Comedian Marga Gomez after a gig at
Josie's Cabaret and Juice Joint.
PHOTOGRAPH BY RICK GERHARTER

NEW YORK, NEW YORK
The commercial TV show hostess Cathay
Che of Party Talk.
PHOTOGRAPH BY TOM MCKITTERICK

NEW YORK, NEW YORK
The "Wrangler" backstage after their performance in Will Rogers
Follies on Broadway. Left to right, John Gamun, Jason Opsahl,
Jerry Mitchell, Troy Britton Johnson.
PHOTOGRAPH BY TOM MCKITTERICK

Out Front and Running

WE ALWAY SAY THAT IF EVERYBODY GOT TO KNOW SOMEONE GAY, THEIR MISCONCEPTIONS ABOUT US WOULD BE MINIMIZED. AND HERE WAS AN OPPORTUNITY FOR US TO GO BEYOND SERVING OUR OWN COMMUNITY.

by Eric Marcus

I T'S A BLAZINGLY BRIGHT, deceptively chilly early spring morning in Central Park. On this morning, like every Saturday morning, no matter what the weather, the men and women of Front Runners New York head south on the park's main drive shortly after 10:00 a.m. for a run of up to six miles.

A quarter-mile behind the main group of 150 pavement-pounders, financial planner Connie Cohrt, arms pumping, back straight, shoulders over hips, and eyes focused on the distance, talks with her friend Andrew Knox, who is jogging slowly alongside her. Connie, 40, tall, thin, with collar-length silver-streaked light brown hair, is the sole racewalker at today's run. Andrew, 25, a compact five-feet-eight, with thinning light brown hair and hazel eyes to match Connie's, is more accustomed to running at the front of the pack.

"During the winter I was training hard for a 15K race," he recalls. "The 40-below-zero windchills and icy conditions did me in." For the time being he's been instructed to take it easy. Sometimes he stops to walk. Connie doesn't break her stride. "I'm training for the Gay Games," she notes. Andrew is more than understanding.

Andrew first joined Front Runners when he moved to New York from Syracuse in 1992 to take a job in the Office of Peace and Justice for the national headquarters of the Episcopal church. "I thought Front Runners would be a healthy atmosphere, a place I could meet gay and lesbian people with whom I shared values," he says. Front Runners was also a place where Andrew thought he might find a boyfriend, and while he has yet to find romance, he has found role models and family who are proud of who they are.

Connie is one of the family members and role models Andrew found. Like Andrew, Connie joined Front Runners because of her desire to be with family. "I could have joined any one of several walking clubs in Manhattan," she explains, "but I wanted a gay and lesbian group because of the feeling of family, of comfort. We spend so much of our time in society-at-large, where I generally feel very comfortable—I'm out at my job—but sometimes it's nice to be in a group that's just gay men and lesbians."

Connie is quick to note that Front Runners is not *exclusively* gay and lesbian. Jeff Singleton and Tina Isselbacher, a heterosexual couple, run with the group, along with their two-year-old daughter Haley, who gets to ride in a running stroller. Andrew recalls, "When Jeff and Tina's daughter was born, the group got a collection together and bought the stroller, along with a pair of baby Nikes. A couple of men in the group knit sweaters for her, and they've had me baby-sit for her."

After the run, Connie and Andrew head back to the church basement where Front Runners meets after the Saturday run for coffee and bagels, announcements, and this week, to do a mass mailing of applications for the group's upcoming annual Gay Pride Run.

Terry Lorden, a theater administrator, sits at the end of a long table stuffing and sealing envelopes. Terry, who is well into his forties, joined Front Runners in 1993, not long after he came out. Like Andrew and Connie, he enjoys the family aspect of Front Runners, but he also thinks that Front Runners helps destroy stereotypes. At least that was his experience last year when he volunteered to work at the Front Runners water table at the New York Marathon.

"There were about 30 of us there at the time and the organizers decided to expand our water stop. So they brought in a large group of New York Telephone volunteers with their kids. Most of us were wearing our Front Runners running gear, so people asked what Front Runners was, and we explained.

"Sometimes you forget that gay and lesbian is such an unusual thing, but you could see in their eyes that this was a startling revelation. A lot of straight people have very stereotyped ideas and they were confronted with the realization that a lot of gay people are just like they are."

Terry explains that at first some of the New York Telephone volunteers manned a separate table, but as the flood of racers poured by, everyone pitched in and worked together. "We always say that if everybody in America got to know someone gay, their reservations and misconceptions about us would be minimized. And here was an opportunity for us to go beyond serving our own community and be goodwill ambassadors to the larger world." With that, Terry went back to the work at hand, slipping another race application into an envelope, this one destined for a point far west of the Hudson.

MIAMI BEACH, FLORIDA
Former kickboxing world champion Lisa Gaylord
on the sands of South Beach.
PHOTOGRAPH BY ALEXIS RODRIGUEZ-DUARTE

SAN FRANCISCO, CALIFORNIA
A gay rodeo participant takes a break.
PHOTOGRAPH BY RICK GERHARTER

MOUNT McKINLEY NATIONAL PARK, ALASKA
Tour guide Karen Jettmar (center) leads topless
lesbians Jill D. Hoelting and Jo Young in telemark skiing
on the snowfields of Mount McKinley.
PHOTOGRAPH BY KAREN JETTMAR AND MIA OXLEY

WEST HOLLYWOOD, CALIFORNIA
Pull ups at the Athletic Club.
PHOTOGRAPH BY BART EVERLY

NEW YORK, NEW YORK
*Ira Rosenbaum, living with AIDS, takes an aquarobics
class at Manhattan Plaza's swimming pool.*
PHOTOGRAPH BY ALLAN CLEAR

NEW YORK, NEW YORK
Laura Moore and April Martin train for the Gay Games.
PHOTOGRAPH BY DONNA BINDER

PORTLAND, OREGON
Members of the Portland Lesbian Choir on a Deschutes
River whitewater rafting expedition.
PHOTOGRAPH BY LINDA KLIEWER

LOS ANGELES, CALIFORNIA
*A high-heel egg race at the Minority AIDS
Project staff picnic.*
PHOTOGRAPH BY BRUCE HUNT

MINNEAPOLIS, MINNESOTA
The Queer Street Patrol training to deter bias crimes at Body Quest Gym.
PHOTOGRAPH BY KEL KELLER

LOS ANGELES, CALIFORNIA
The LA Blades, during a sixteen-game winning streak, defeating the L.A. Police Department.
PHOTOGRAPH BY TOM MCKITTERICK

NEW YORK, NEW YORK
*An American samurai. Debi Farmer, here
seen on a Roosevelt Island rooftop, studies
Japanese Kendo at the Doshikan Dojo.*
PHOTOGRAPH BY YASUHIDE JOJU

PHOENIX, ARIZONA
*Gene Mikilenka of Houston, a member of the Texas
chapter of the International Gay Rodeo
Association, at a bronc-riding event.*
PHOTOGRAPH BY PATSY LYNCH

SAN FRANCISCO, CALIFORNIA
Boxer Gina Guidi with her trainer, Rio, at King's Gym in East Oakland. She is hoping to fight professionally, despite huge opposition.
PHOTOGRAPH BY JILL POSENER

WASHINGTON, D.C.
*Members of the D.C. Strokes, the only gay crew
team in America, sweep the Potomac River.*
PHOTOGRAPH BY PATSY LYNCH

LOS ANGELES, CALIFORNIA
*Olympic Gold Medal diver Greg Louganis with
Brutus (foreground) and Donna.*
PHOTOGRAPH BY GREG GORMAN

AUSTIN, TEXAS

Tony Johnson of the TriAngels, a gay and lesbian skydiving team, comes down "under canopy." Made up of 15 members, the TriAngels planned to jump three members onto the opening ceremonies of Gay Games IV in New York City.

PHOTOGRAPHS BY JANA BIRCHUM

Jaquie Roberts practices with her jumpmaster before her first dive.

Mike Leggitt takes the big leap backward.

Kirsten Johnson's face says it all.

Joyce Gayles is congratulated after her first dive by her team members.

Tony Johnson and Kent Gilliam together in free fall.

Ron Blissett in bliss on terra firma.

Kirsten Johnson and her lover, Lisa Lyle, in a victory embrace.

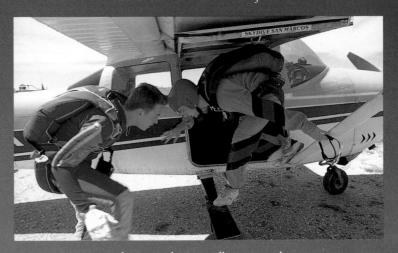

Tony Johnson and Kent Gilliam try a dry run.

ATLANTA, GEORGIA
Jeff Ames takes a silent cue from Garry Turner
at a deaf bowling league exhibition.
PHOTOGRAPH BY SCOTT AUERBACH

CHICAGO, ILLINOIS
Partners Karla Shelton and Angela Schmidt performing
at a bodybuilding exhibition benefit for the Gay
Games' Team Chicago.
PHOTOGRAPH BY GERARD SANTOS

NEW YORK, NEW YORK
*Over 28,000 attended the opening ceremonies for Gay Games IV
held at Lawrence A. Wien Stadium/Baker Field.*
PHOTOGRAPH BY MICK HICKS

NEW YORK, NEW YORK
*Track and field athletes Kenneth Parish, 100-meter gold medalist Rebecca Weinberg,
and 400-meter silver and 200-meter bronze winner Alvin Pickettay.*
PHOTOGRAPH BY PETER LEVASSEUR

NEW YORK, NEW YORK
*Men's diving competition at Asphalt Greens during
Gay Games IV.*
PHOTOGRAPH BY TOM BIANCHI

Emancipation Day

"NOW LET'S ALL JOIN HANDS, AND REMEMBER THOSE WHO CANNOT BE WITH US. THEY ARE WITH US, SOMEWHERE, LISTENING FOR THEIR NAMES." IN A SLOW STEADY VOICE, LEHMAN SINGS: "WHEN SHE CALLS ME, I WILL ANSWER."

by Renee Graham

BILLIE HOLIDAY caresses "God Bless the Child," coaxing tears and heartache between the scratch and hiss of a 78-speed record. The thick, heavy aroma of okra and tomato, cornbread and collards, and the rice, beans, and ham hocks Southerners call "Hoppin' John" wafts from the kitchen, wrapping the room in a warm, familiar embrace. Sunlight winks through the trees into a room aglow with candles, one for each of the eight women kneeling around a small mahogany table.

On this New Year's Day, as her family has done for more than a half-century, Twyla Greer celebrates "Emancipation Day," commemorating Jan. 1, 1863, when President Abraham Lincoln's Emancipation Proclamation ended slavery in America. From the foods and herb teas, even to the echo of Billie Holiday's peerless voice, much in this ritual of remembrance has remained the same from Greer's childhood. Yet in the seven years she and her lover, Adele Lehman, have opened their Boston

home to share her family tradition with their friends, Greer has also made it her own.

"Hoppin' John," her grandmother's recipe with cowpeas soaked in vinegar, is now called "Hoppin' Jane." The call-and-response readings and spiritual songs passed from one generation to the next are now led by women. And the prayers, the words of reverence once reserved for family, are now extended to this circle of kindred women joined by their shared strength and common love.

"May we all continue to be blessed with the joy of each other," Greer says, before sipping a cup of honey-lemon tea from which all the women will eventually drink. The shared cup is a symbol of communion, an emblem of their unity.

"Now let's all join hands, and remember those who cannot be with us," Greer says. "They are with us, somewhere, listening for their names." In a slow steady voice, Lehman begins to sing:

"When She calls me, I will answer
"When She calls me, I will answer
"When She calls me, I will answer
"I'll be somewhere, listening for my name."

Soon, the tiny room fills with the rich voices of women. The singing continues as each of the women recalls the name of someone they have lost—a father murdered by an unknown assailant, a sister lost to breast cancer, a grandparent ravaged by age, a beautiful young friend destroyed by AIDS.

They remember those who have died by domestic, racial, and anti-gay violence. Some quote poignant passages from favorite books and journals.

And on this day of emancipation, they also evoke the memory of those—including Audre Lorde, Pat Parker, and Mabel Hampton—who shone light and understanding on the lives of those like themselves, women who love women.

Still, this is not a solemn day in the Greer-Lehman household. It is a celebration of those who have supported and sustained them, a celebration of surviving yet another year, and, above all, a celebration of family.

"Emancipation Day has always been very special to me, and it only makes sense for me to share it with the people I am closest to," Greer says. "For me, this has always been a family holiday, and these women are as much my family as anyone could be."

All the readings read, all the songs sung, all that is left is a tantalizing array of foods. Greer blows out her candle, and each women extinguishes the candle to her left. "Let's live this year laughing often, caring always, and loving fiercely," Greer declares. "Now it's time for Hoppin' Jane, and as my mama used to say, 'You got to serve yourselves, 'cause there ain't no guests in my house.'"

They run into the kitchen, laughing and hugging. And just above the din, Billie's frayed wail blesses these women who have found their own.

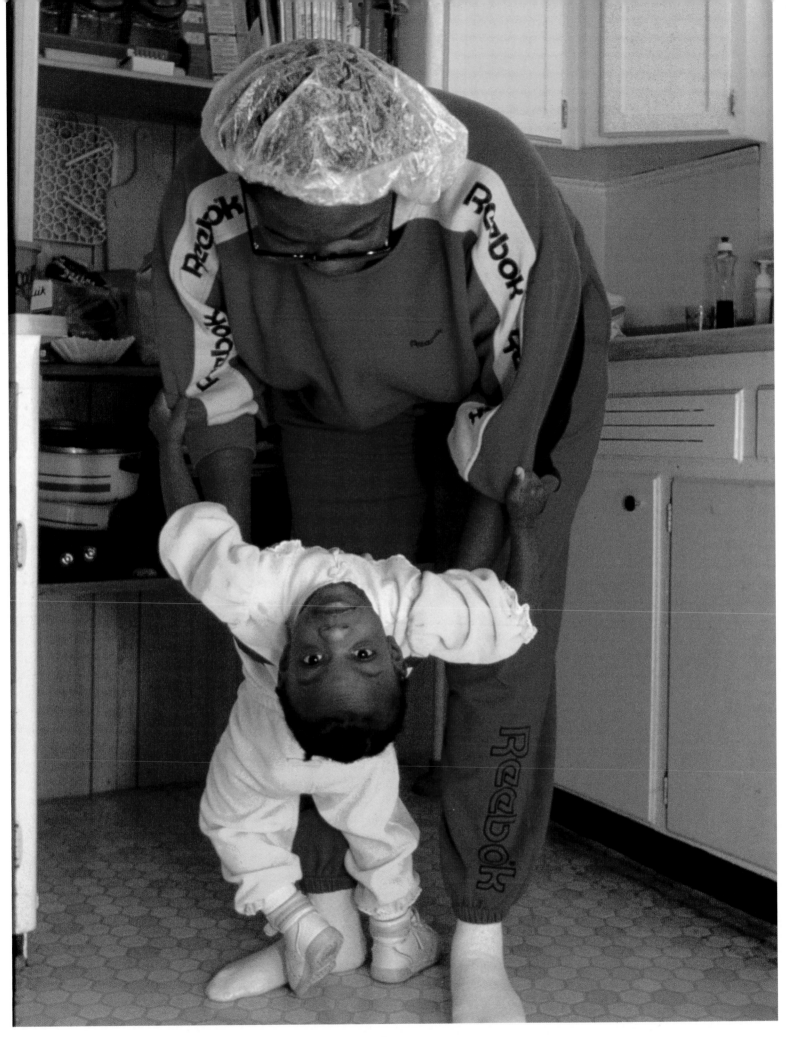

LINCOLN, NEBRASKA
Iris Johnson-Aki and her daughter Mariah.
PHOTOGRAPH BY ROBIN TRIMARCHI

BRONX, NEW YORK
Peter Ott teaches daughter Ariana to play the piano.
PHOTOGRAPH BY LIMOR INBAR

TAMPA, FLORIDA
Lesbian Avengers relaxing at home.
PHOTOGRAPH BY DONNA BINDER

SAN FRANCISCO, CALIFORNIA
Lesbian moms Lisa Orta and Karen Rust with their son Gary Rust-Orta at Camp It Up, a camp for children and parents of alternative families.
PHOTOGRAPH BY PHYLLIS CHRISTOPHER

NEW YORK, NEW YORK
Couples with children signing up under the domestic partnership agreement.
PHOTOGRAPH BY LES STONE

PHILADELPHIA, PENNSYLVANIA
Doria and Fawn cuddle up in a friend's apartment.
PHOTOGRAPH BY AMY LEIGH STEINER

*Members of Womontown, a lesbian community in the
seventy-five-year-old neighborhood of Dutch Hill, hold
their annual yard sale.*
PHOTOGRAPH BY ANEAL VOHRA

PROVINCETOWN, MASSACHUSETTS
Friends and family at a Fourth of July celebration.
PHOTOGRAPH BY JOSEPH DELVECCHIO

WASHINGTON, D.C.
Jane Dolkart blows out her birthday candles
at a party given by friends.
PHOTOGRAPH BY JEB

SAN FRANCISCO, CALIFORNIA
Friends gather for an early morning dog run at Bernal Heights.
PHOTOGRAPH BY JILL POSENER

SAN FRANCISCO, CALIFORNIA
*Sean Sasser, public policy coordinator for YES (Youth Empowerment
Services), and AIDS educator Pedro Zamora. Both appear on
MTV's* The Real World.
PHOTOGRAPH BY KEN PROBST

*Rob Moss with his mother, Doris, who has been caring for
him since he became disabled by AIDS-related illnesses.*
PHOTOGRAPH BY PETER ROSS

NEW YORK, NEW YORK
Michael E. Lasser and Doug Robinson with their
six-year-old son, Zachary, on their way to school.
PHOTOGRAPH BY TOM MCKITTERICK

OVETT, MISSISSIPPI

Brenda and Wanda Henson, founders of Camp Sister Spirit, the beleagured feminist retreat.

PHOTOGRAPH BY RICK GERHARTER

KNOXVILLE, TENNESSEE

A family tree reveals a family secret.

PHOTOGRAPH BY RUSTY SMART

This is my great-grandfather, Robert Houston Barnett (r.) & his unidentified "friend," circa 1890. Grandaddy got married a few years later, raised a fine family. But he occasionally took off on long weekends.

This is my great, grand partner, Charles Frank Hawkins, Jr. (l.) & me, circa 1990. We fell in love when we were 13. Eighteen years later, we occasionally take off on long weekends together.

GLEN ROCK, NEW JERSEY
Julie and Dylan Zuckerman with cranky, the cat.
PHOTOGRAPH BY LIMOR INBAR

Mayor

"I HAD A FARMER COME OUT TO ME AT THE MAID-RITE, HE SAT DOWN AT THE COUNTER AND ASKED ABOUT PLUGGING WATER WELLS. AT THE END HE SAID, 'I REALLY ADMIRE YOU FOR WHAT YOU'VE DONE, BECAUSE I'M ONE.'"

by Chandler Burr

B ILL CREWS, MAYOR, Melbourne, Iowa.

"Melbourne's a little town in between Des Moines and Marshalltown on Highway 330. In the last census, it was population 669. We prefer to say 'around 700.' I became mayor 'cause nobody else wanted to do it, pretty much. They asked me to. I'd only just moved there with my partner of fifteen years, Steve Kehoe. But you know, 'elected official,' of course I couldn't resist. I ran for reelection in '85, got 100 percent of the vote. All fifty-seven people who voted, voted for me.

"Two years ago I ran in the Republican primary for Iowa State Senate. I'm a Republican, from before the fascists took over. I believe in limited government. But I'm on one side of the party. I'm pro-choice. I've always been. My dad grew up in the South, one of the reasons he was a Republican. He was very active in racial equality issues, and he knew what the Democrats were when he was growing up: segregationists. Till it kind of flip-flopped.

"He was killed in a car accident twenty years ago.

"Steve wasn't ready to be out, so I ran for the Senate kind of closeted. But it always bothered me, and it didn't work anyway. Early in my campaign a conservative religious person called and asked me if I was gay, and I said it shouldn't make a difference, and he said, nastily, 'Well, I'll just assume you are.'

"That was when we finally realized we had to be out. So we made plans to come out at the March on Washington.

"The Gay and Lesbian Victory Fund had a brunch for out elected officials the day before the March, called 'Recognizing Our Own.' I got a standing ovation as the newest out elected official. Jeff Schmalz wrote about me in the Sunday New York Times. I got a hug from David Mixner. Rod and Bob Jackson-Paris were there. They took pictures, and I stood between Barney Frank and Gerry Studds.

"The Des Moines Register—a statewide paper—on Monday's front page had a color picture of the March, and below it, it read 'The unofficial leader of the Iowa group appeared to be Melbourne mayor Bill Crews.' And I think that was what caught the eye of the vandals who spray-painted our house. Driving up the hill Tuesday we saw the house, and we got this sinking feeling. They wrote 'Melbourne hates gays, get out.' And 'Queers aren't welcome,' and they spelled it 'arn't.'

"The next day we had six TV crews waiting for us.

"I think there was universal condemnation of the vandalism in the town. We had our annual Spring Cleanup Day scheduled for that Saturday. As mayor I direct that, and it went off without a hitch. There was nothing but support.

"Well, there were comments from the guys at the bar—there's just one bar—that we were just using the town. People were getting harassed for being from the town with the gay mayor. My neighbor across the street who sells farm implements told me that. He would say, 'Yeah, I know him, and he's a nice guy.' And that usually shut 'em up.

"We don't blame the town for the vandalism. Melbourne doesn't hate gays.

"I'm active in my church, the United Methodists. My dad was a United Methodist minister. We're losing our minister over this because she's been so supportive. Two families left. But this has strengthened my spirituality. Jesus preached inclusiveness and acceptance, and since God made me this way, it's not a sin. Our minister only preached one sermon on 'homosexuality,' and after that she was just preaching about being a good Christian, don't judge others. People blame her for bringing it up all the time, but it's just that they're hearing her and realizing they need to apply this to me.

"I had a farmer come out to me at the Maid-Rite, he sat down at the counter and asked, about plugging water wells. At the end he said 'I really admire you for what you've done, because I'm one.' One time I called the septic tank installer, and his wife said, 'By the way, I think that's a great thing you did.'

"We'll win. It'll be one person at a time, though. You learn your friend's gay, a family member, you think, 'Well, what's the matter with that?'"

MELBOURNE, IOWA
Mayor Bill Crews visits with a constituent.
PHOTOGRAPH BY PETER ROSS

NEW YORK, NEW YORK
Gilbert Baker sews the one-mile-long, thirty-feet-wide
Rainbow Flag at the Raise the Rainbow workshop.
PHOTOGRAPH BY MICK HICKS

EUGENE, OREGON
Joy at the defeat of anti-gay legislation, Measure 9.
PHOTOGRAPH BY DONNA BINDER

ONE AID[S]
EVERY 1
MINUTE

BETHESDA, MARYLAND
Bringing the message to the National Institutes of Health.
PHOTOGRAPH BY DONNA BINDER

NEW YORK, NEW YORK
The Pink Panthers, an anti-gay-bashing patrol.
PHOTOGRAPH BY T.L. LITT

126

New York, New York
*Queer Nation's answer to Ross Perot's
openly-homophobic campaign.*
PHOTOGRAPH BY RON HAVIV

NEW YORK, NEW YORK
Protest at St. James Roman Catholic Church after a gay-bashing
in Brooklyn and a homophobic letter delivered by a bishop.
PHOTOGRAPH BY DONNA BINDER

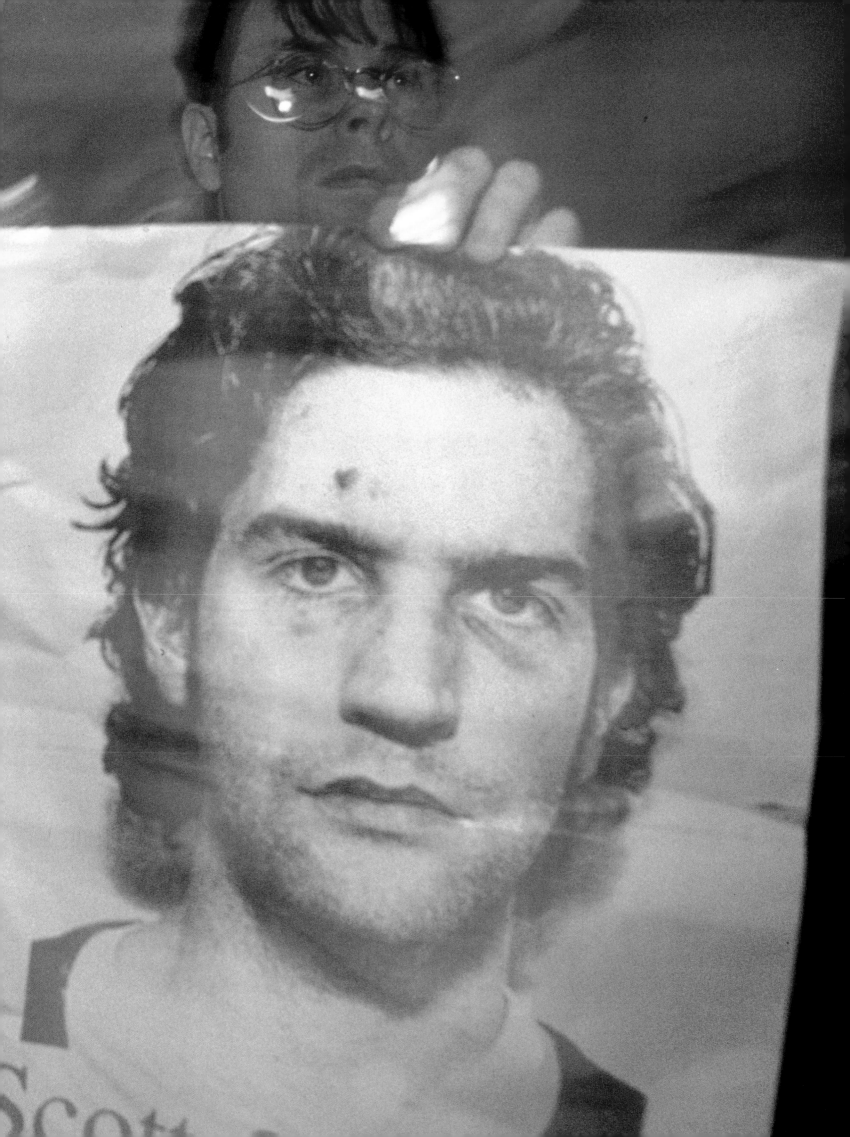

WASHINGTON, D.C.
As true now as it was in Washington in 1979.
PHOTOGRAPH BY BETTYE LANE

WASHINGTON, D.C.
*Michael Callen and others at a 1983 march in
Washington for AIDS research.*
PHOTOGRAPH BY BETTYE LANE

WASHINGTON, D.C.
The Mattachine Society marching bravely in front of the White
House on behalf of the "nation's second largest minority." 1965.
PHOTOGRAPH BY BETTMAN ARCHIVES

NEW YORK, NEW YORK
Anita Bryant's anti-gay campaign is answered at a
Christopher Street Pride Day in 1977.
PHOTOGRAPH BY BETTYE LANE

WASHINGTON, D.C.
David Mixner (right) at the Democratic National Convention.
PHOTOGRAPH BY T.L. LITT

Tom Chiola and his mother, Faye, celebrate his victory as the first
openly gay Democratic Circuit Court nominee in Illinois history.
PHOTOGRAPH BY PETER ROSS

SAN FRANCISCO, CALIFORNIA
A thousand mourners gather inside and outside Glide
Memorial Church at the funeral of writer Randy
Shilts on February 22, 1994.
PHOTOGRAPH BY RICK GERHARTER

WASHINGTON, D.C.
Sabrina Sojourner lobbies in 1993 to end
the ban on gays in the military.
PHOTOGRAPH BY PATSY LYNCH

NEW YORK, NEW YORK
Dancing in the streets during the International Dyke March, part of Stonewall 25.
PHOTOGRAPH BY LISA KAHANE

NEW YORK, NEW YORK
The alternative Stonewall 25 March on Fifth Avenue, led by ACT UP.
PHOTOGRAPH BY LISA KAHANE

SAN FRANCISCO, CALIFORNIA
*Protest following the lenient treatment of Dan White, who
assassinated San Francisco mayor George Moscone and
beloved gay supervisor Harvey Milk in their offices in 1978.*
PHOTOGRAPH BY MICK HICKS

San Francisco, California

San Francisco supervisor Harvey Britt, successor to Harvey Milk, announces his run for Congress in front of City Hall, scene of Milk's death, in March, 1987.

PHOTOGRAPH BY MARC GELLER

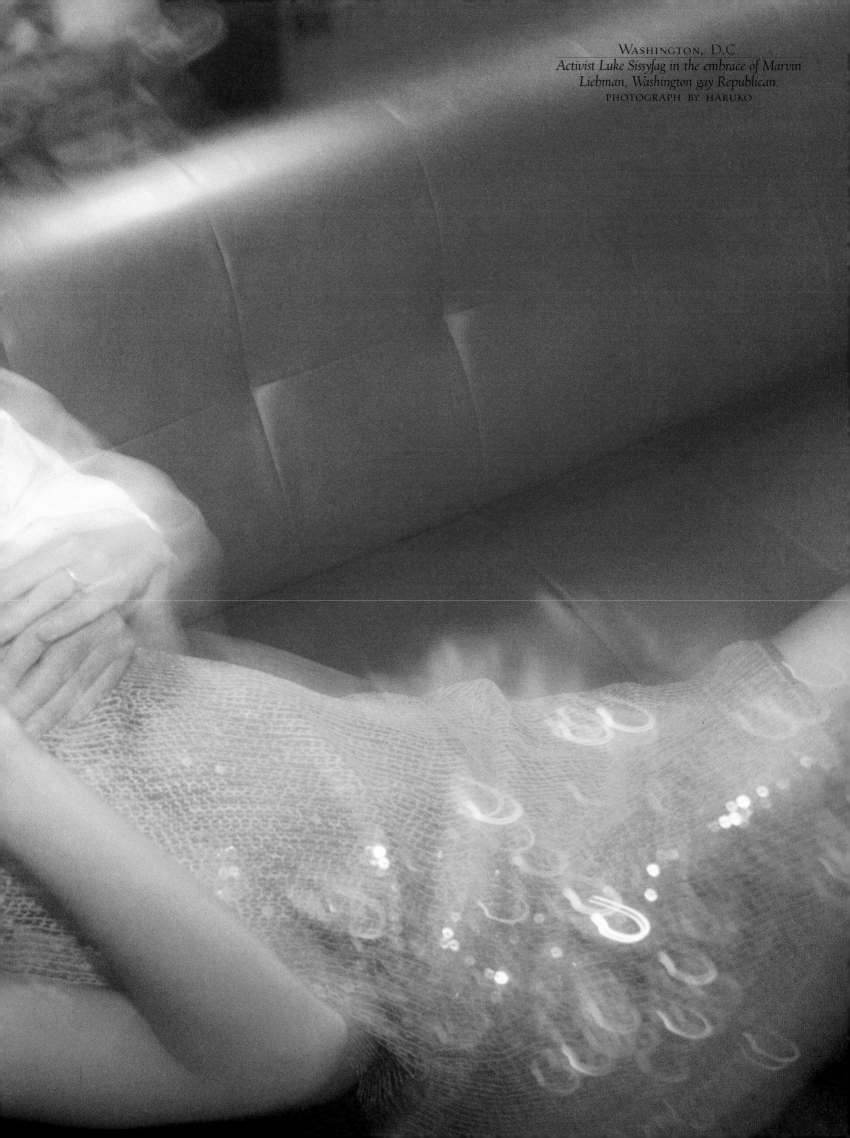

My Cupboard Full of Gods

THEY WORE FABULOUS GOWNS IN GLORIOUS COLORS AND THEY ALL LIVED IN EQUAL OPPORTUNITY HEAVEN, EATING P'TAO-T'AO, THE PEACHES OF IMMORTALITY, SIPPING WINE AND HANGING OUT. THE ULTIMATE GAY DESTINY.

by *Lily Eng*

EIGHT immortals looked over me when I was growing up in Jersey City, New Jersey. They lived in a cupboard in my mother's bedroom on the second floor of our laundry shop on Jackson Avenue. They shared space with gossip magazines and a Statue of Liberty pencil sharpener, the kind you buy at Woolworth's.

My parents, immigrants from China, were not religious, but they were superstitious. No one talked God; conversations centered on spirits. The cupboard served as an altar for the beautiful porcelain figures; spiritual superheroes, each one either represented a virtue or had a knack for accomplishing something godlike. My relatives and Chinese friends all had a set of the immortals too.

The Taoist deities stood in a half-circle, facing front. Han Chung-Li, a smiling old man, represented happiness. Chang-Kuo Lao owned a compact traveling donkey that raced across thousands of miles in a day and folded up in a neat packet for safe storage. Ho-Hsien-Ku, the lone goddess, waved a lotus, a fruit that induced

dreaminess. They wore fabulous gowns in glorious colors and they all lived in equal opportunity heaven, eating P'Tao-T'ao, the peaches of immortality, sipping wine and hanging out together. The ultimate gay destiny.

Every Saturday I faithfully dusted the tiny gods with a Handiwipe. They fit comfortably in my hands, yet they were big enough so I could see the expressions on their faces. They were in heavenly bliss, even though their entire world was in a cupboard. I envied the gods. Porcelain of body and soul, they were content, their search for spirituality complete.

As a girl dusting seven gods and one goddess, I didn't think about faith, spirituality, gay or straight, heaven or hell. That was too difficult to comprehend. Instead, I wondered whether God was made of fragile porcelain.

Christianity was a mystery, though my sisters and brother attended a United Methodist Church. There they learned about the Gospel, baptisms, and the body of Christ. Sometimes my parents excused me from Sunday School and church. I figured it was reward for my great cleaning job—I had a way with the nooks, crannies and altars. Truth was, my parents couldn't get me out of bed, so I never attended enough classes to pass Sunday School and get baptized like my sisters and brother.

During services where spirituality meshed with food and drink, my siblings sipped grape juice and ate bread. Unbaptized, I settled for a tap on the head from the minister and still wondered about God. Does God eat toast and

drink grape juice too? What is it about God, food, and spirituality?

By the time I reached high school, God was friend and stranger, a being who supposedly protected me, a being who was unknown. I attended an all-girls Catholic high school, where nuns doled out the Gospel, Christ and faith in daily homework assignments. Each day opened with a prayer, and every big event was blessed with a church service, including Bingo. Gays and lesbians didn't exist, at least not in Catholic school.

Catholic churches kept their own altars, huge cupboards overflowing with porcelain Jesuses and Marys. Sealed in giant test-tubes, they, too, looked heavenly, and they certainly didn't share their space with any souvenirs. I found myself praying to the tubes for better grades, a better allowance, and for my chemistry partner to notice me. I wondered, "Does God like gays and lesbians?" Maria, my chemistry partner, noticed me, and we've been together more than fifteen years. God does like us.

Nowadays I don't belong to a church or a temple or study any particular book. But my faith leans toward Christianity, and I am partial to Love Thy Neighbor. I pray almost daily. It's almost like my soul is communicating with my mind and body, and it comforts me to talk about my hopes and dreams.

Spirituality is a lifetime search, and I'm still exploring other faiths. It keeps the soul healthy and open-minded. The immortals are still alive at my mother's house. I don't know who is dusting them now.

NEW YORK, NEW YORK
*Choreographer Stanley Love rehearses with
his dance troupe.*
PHOTOGRAPH BY KLAUS SCHONWIESE

SEATTLE, WASHINGTON
*Angelique Von Holle (center) blesses the traditional
Jewish Sabbath meal.*
PHOTOGRAPH BY DANA SCHUERHOLZ

BOYDS, MARYLAND
*Reverend Ken Ehrke at the new Open Door
Metropolitan Community Church.*
PHOTOGRAPH BY LENNY GONZALEZ

ATLANTA, GEORGIA
Jan Barlow sings and weeps at a funeral for her lover.
She held a separate service, since the family did not
approve of the couple's love.
PHOTOGRAPH BY ADAM TAYLOR

SAN FRANCISCO, CALIFORNIA
1993 *Candlelight vigil for people with AIDS.*
PHOTOGRAPH BY LISA FISHER

KANSAS CITY, MISSOURI
1993. A viewing of the AIDS Quilt.
PHOTOGRAPH BY ANEAL VOHRA

SAN FRANCISCO, CALIFORNIA
A gay monk meditating at the Hartford Street Zen Center in the heart of the Castro district. The Center runs an adjoining hospice for those with long-term illnesses.
PHOTOGRAPH BY RICK GERHARTER

BATON ROUGE, LOUISIANA
Holistic healing through touch with Fabian (right).
PHOTOGRAPH BY KEYTH BOURDIER

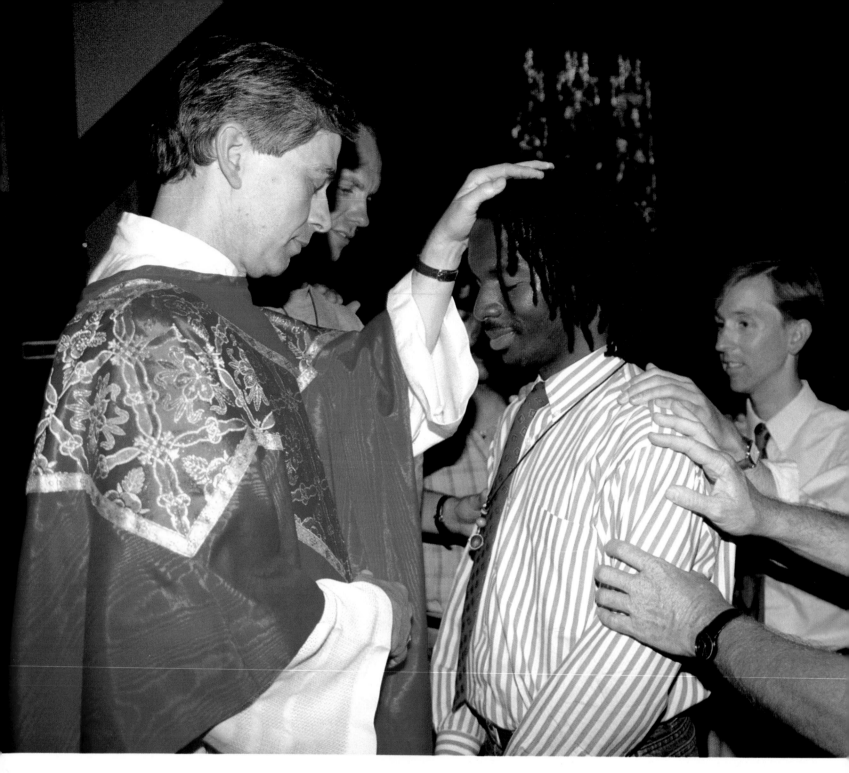

WASHINGTON, DC
A weekly healing ceremony at All Souls Episcopal Church
for those with AIDS and those affected by it.
PHOTOGRAPH BY PATSY LYNCH

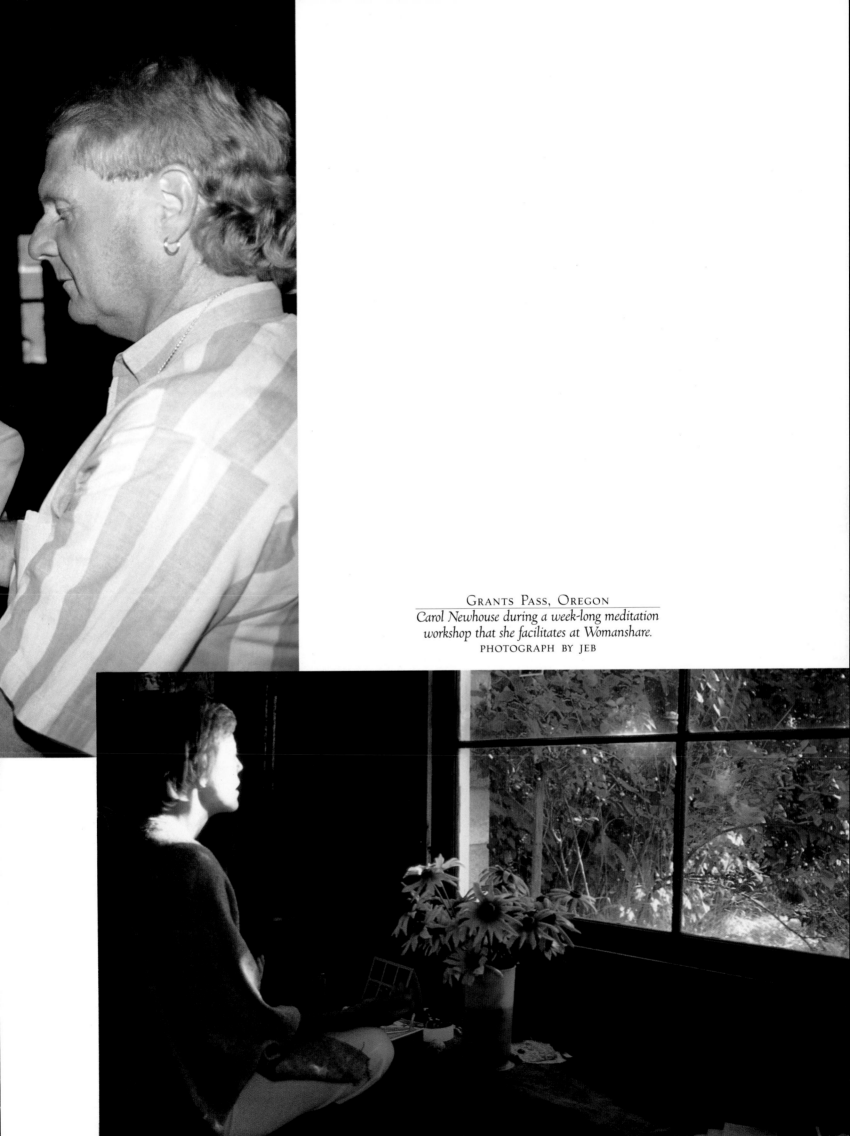

GRANTS PASS, OREGON
*Carol Newhouse during a week-long meditation
workshop that she facilitates at Womanshare.*
PHOTOGRAPH BY JEB

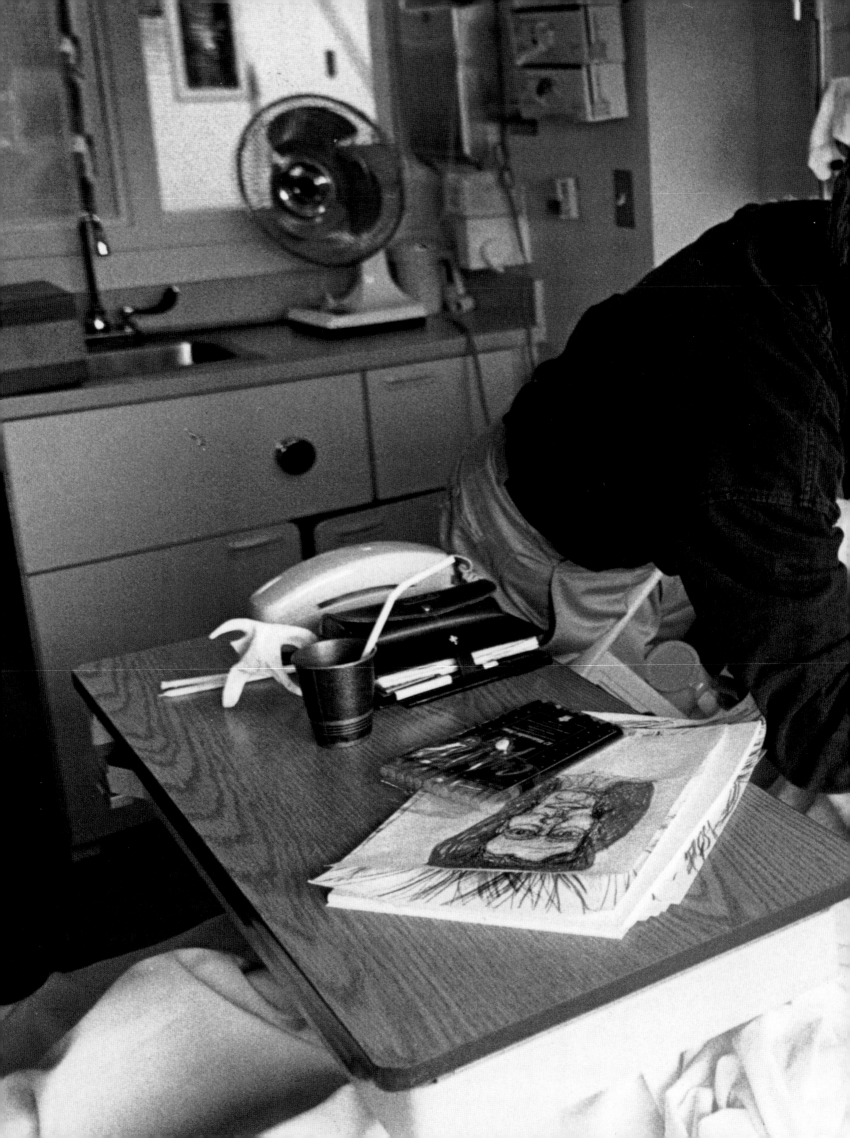

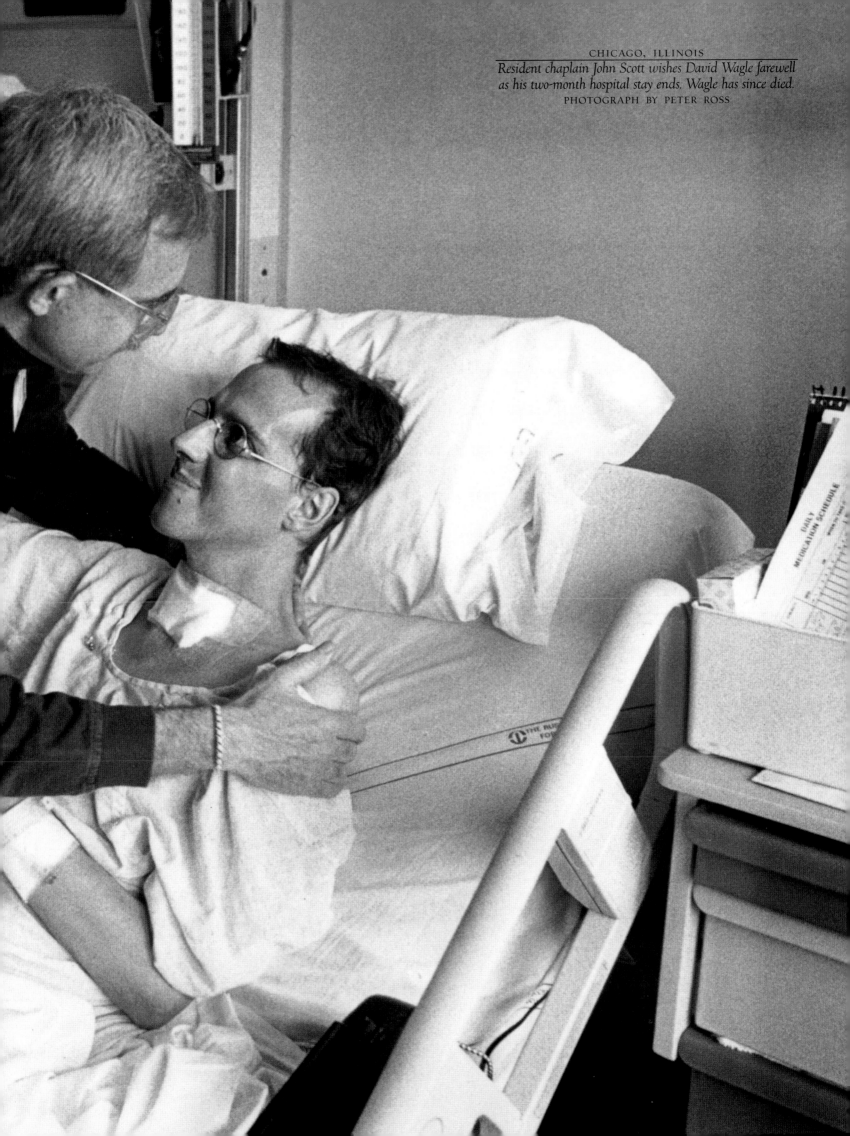

CHICAGO, ILLINOIS
Resident chaplain John Scott wishes David Wagle farewell
as his two-month hospital stay ends. Wagle has since died.
PHOTOGRAPH BY PETER ROSS

LIBERTY, TENNESSEE

The Radical Faeries celebrate their annual Rite of Spring at Short Mountain, including a lesbian wedding ceremony.

PHOTOGRAPH BY PETER LIEN

HOUSTON, TEXAS
*Satya Sheperd and Cindy Freeman lead a lunar eclipse ritual
celebrating the healing power of women.*
PHOTOGRAPH BY SHARON STEWART

GRAND CANYON, ARIZONA
In still flight on the south rim of the Grand Canyon.
PHOTOGRAPH BY CURTIS A. PEREZ

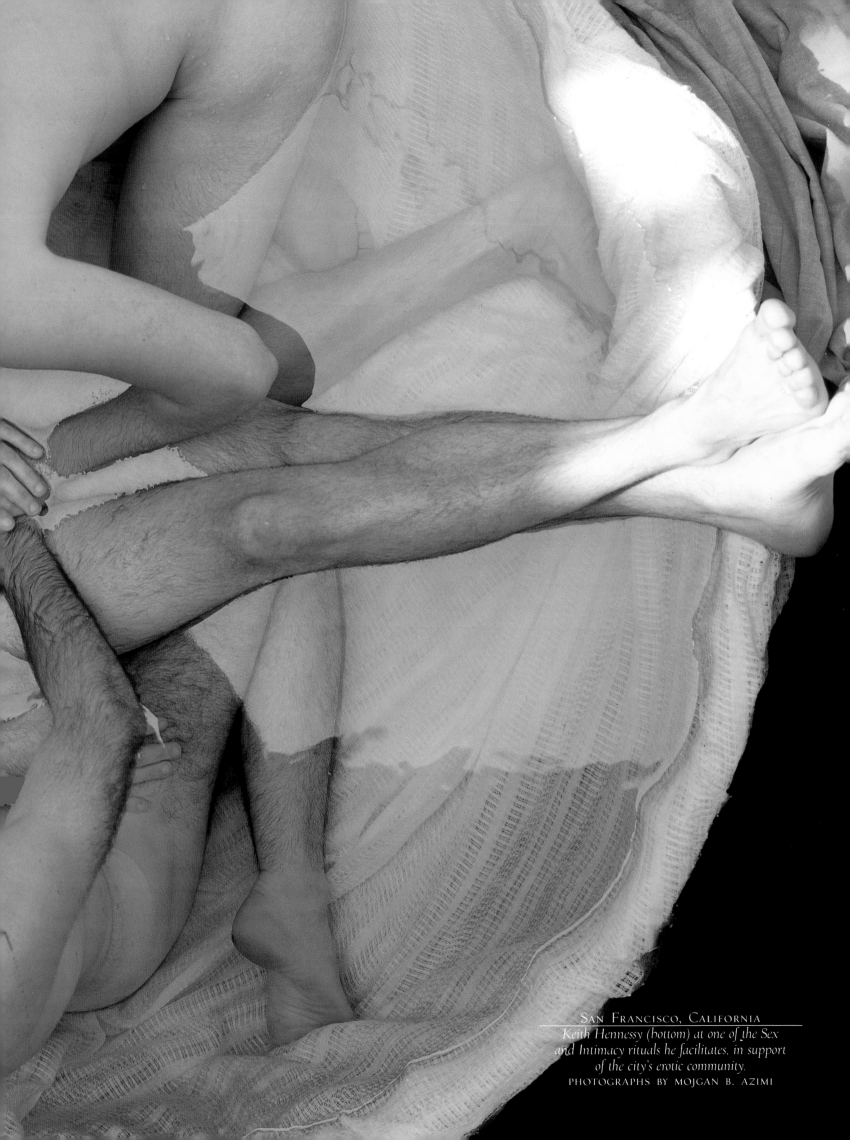

SAN FRANCISCO, CALIFORNIA
*Keith Hennessy (bottom) at one of the Sex
and Intimacy rituals he facilitates, in support
of the city's erotic community.*
PHOTOGRAPHS BY MOJGAN B. AZIMI

The Return of the Dweeb

IT WAS AN EDGY, SELF-INDULGENT CARNIVAL OF SOULS, PERVADED BY A DISTINCT SENSE OF PHYSICALITY THAT FELT LIKE A SECOND WIND OF HORMONES. THE MEMORIES ALONE STILL HAVE ME DUCKING FOR COVER.

by Michael Musto

I WAS NEVER INTERNATIONAL Male catalog material—in fact, I've always been somewhat hunched over and unsightly looking—but in my fervid imagination I pictured the gay world to be one where that wouldn't matter at all, if you had the coquetry and charm to cover it up. At gay bars, I was sure, a bubbly personality mixed with a few sardonic remarks and quotes from old Joan Crawford movies could instantly make one the belle of the ball.

Obviously I was in for the rudest awakening since realizing that my new Barbie doll wouldn't make me the most popular boy in the neighborhood. Coming out in New York in the late '70s, I quickly found out that no one goes to bars looking for sassy personalities to take home; they want to get laid, and definitely not by some smart-talking nerd.

That's why it was particularly heartening when—after years and years of empty dance cards—the late '80s finally came around with a different spin on the old mating game. AIDS

had made its first horrific impact and traumatized people into thinking they could never have sex again. But now we were accepting that the crisis was here for the duration, and learning to educate ourselves towards a leap into safer (as opposed to no) sex. Body fascism wasn't fully imagined yet—that extremist concept wouldn't catch on until a few more years into this new sexual revolution. Instead, an East Village ethos of angry activism had arisen, whereby the right spirit and political stance really did count for something in the meat-market value system. Cute was still worshiped, of course, but if you weren't a potential porn star, having a fighter's soul definitely added points. Plus, people were so horny from having not done it for so long that their standards had become a little more lenient.

Catering explicitly to this new sensibility was Rock 'n' Roll Fag Bar, a party held every Tuesday at the World, that run-down, two-floor ex-wedding hall in the far reaches of "Alphabetland" (the most treacherous part of the East Village). As run by a 6'6", bald, defiant drag queen named Dean Johnson, the event boasted an anything-goes atmosphere that elevated the ragtag and celebrated the down-and-dirty. Not only didn't you have to be a catalog model, but you didn't even have to sport East Village chic, as long as you liked to whoop it up with a depraved and festive loudness.

The deejay played a bracing hodgepodge of glam rock, new-wave kitsch, and current

dance tracks—everything from Marc Bolan to a Sinéad O'Connor/Karen Finley mix. Go-go boys posed and pranced onstage in their Calvins—the first sighting of this phenomenon in clubland—and they were an eclectic bunch, with even a few skanky types, one of whom I think was Johnson's boyfriend. And round 1:30 A.M., the stage was taken over by some kind of crazed performance—often Johnson and his band, the Weenies, singing that lilting ditty, "Fuck You," other times local drag hags doing age-old lip-synch—and people would actually watch. Then, in a dilapidated upstairs back room, marked by the sounds of groping, moaning, and air-kissing, the clientele would give a more private hand to their personal icons (though sadly, the monitors were generally too busy working the room to work on the room).

It was an edgy, self-indulgent carnival of souls, pervaded by a distinct sense of physicality that felt like a second wind of hormones. The memories alone still have me ducking for cover. Someone once almost broke my back while jumping me to the floor as a greeting; another guy ritualistically enjoyed the game of being pretend-gang-raped on the stairway; and yet another lug once impulsively pinned me to the wall and ended up vomiting all over my living room, hours later.

Now, of course, it's back to the '70s ethic of superficial chic—no pecs, no sex—and once again I'm the dweeb in the corner.

NEW YORK, NEW YORK
Wigstock, the annual one-day drag festival at Tompkins Square Park.
PHOTOGRAPH BY HAIM ARIAV

NEW YORK, NEW YORK
Go-go girls at the Clit Club.
PHOTOGRAPH BY T.L. LITT

CHICAGO, ILLINOIS

Contestants in the 1993 International Mr.
Leather contest held at the Aragon Ballroom.
PHOTOGRAPH BY JASON SMITH

SAN FRANCISCO, CALIFORNIA
Queer punks Shanna (right) and Mr. Quijas
at Fort Sunston Beach.
PHOTOGRAPH BY CHLOE SHERMAN

MINNEAPOLIS, MINNESOTA
Friday night dancing at District 200,
a queer youth center.
PHOTOGRAPH BY KEL KELLER

SAN FRANCISCO, CALIFORNIA
Susie Fought ferries a couple home.
PHOTOGRAPH BY JILL POSENER

PROVINCETOWN, MASSACHUSETTS
Leathermen out at night.
PHOTOGRAPH BY BROOKS KRAFT

LOS ANGELES, CALIFORNIA
The first gay and lesbian senior prom in the Los Angeles Unified School District.
Top left, Christina rents a tux. Top right, Jake and Vincent read the program.
Below left, Rachel, Alex, and Tommy; below right, Ricardo, Mathew,
Christina and Josh.
PHOTOGRAPH BY DONNA BINDER

NEW YORK, NEW YORK
West Indian gays party at the Shelter in Manhattan.
PHOTOGRAPH BY C.T. WEMPLE

SAN FRANCISCO, CALIFORNIA
Connie Champagne and cast backstage during
an adaptation of Valley of the Dolls.
PHOTOGRAPH BY MARC GELLER

ROCKY MOUNTAINS, COLORADO
Jenny soaps up during a camping trip in the Rockies.
PHOTOGRAPH BY WHITNEY ROBBINS

PALM SPRINGS, CALIFORNIA
Julie and Joy poolside at the Riviera Hotel in Palm Springs over the 1994 Dinah Shore Weekend.
PHOTOGRAPH BY SUNNY BAK

NEW YORK, NEW YORK
*Playing Scrabble at the Gay and
Lesbian Community Center*
PHOTOGRAPH BY DONNA BINDER

WEST HOLLYWOOD, CALIFORNIA
Boys poolside at the Athletic Club.
PHOTOGRAPH BY BART EVERLY

NEW YORK, NEW YORK
*Performer Lypsinka at the 1993 Wigstock
celebration in Tompkins Square Park.*
PHOTOGRAPH BY HAIM ARIAV

BOSTON, MASSACHUSETTS
Two-step night at the Ramrod.
PHOTOGRAPH BY WILLIAM MOREE

SAN FRANCISCO, CALIFORNIA
Sisters of Perpetual Indulgence, Hellina Handbasket
and Sister X, who has since died
of AIDS, passing out condoms on the cable cars.
PHOTOGRAPH BY JILL POSENER

That Army of Lovers

THIRTY YEARS LATER, BOUNCING ALONG ON ANOTHER BUS, STARING OUTSIDE AT THE LIGHTENING SKY AND AT MYSELF IN THE WINDOW, I REMEMBERED THAT EARLY LOVE, THAT BREATHLESS ATTENTION TO EVERY DETAIL OF HER.

by Kate Clinton

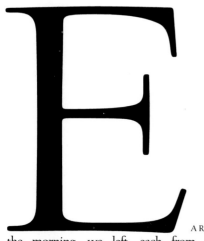

EARLY IN the morning, we left, each from darkened houses, deep blue sky giving way to light. We wore layers—winter coats, sweaters, long socks, flat shoes. Our yawns hung frosted in the cold morning air. We jostled, shifted from foot to foot, stared wide-eyed at nothing, bumped into each other, sleepy, waking.

The school bus yellow shocked us into motion. Its door folding open, we each managed the long reach of the first step, then the next and back down the aisle, shuffling quietly, shifting out of backpacks, sliding into a seat. The bus lurched forward, out of first gear, laboring noisily into second, then third to the next stop.

Rocking forward, I looked out the window, then settled back into the stop. She was there! I held my breath, watched her as she waited in line to board, all leaning forward and quiet. I lost her for a moment as she stepped up, then her precious head appeared, eyes darting from

under her knit hat, looking for a vacant seat. Looking for me? She started down the aisle, hesitated by an open seat as the bus pitched forward. Steadied, she continued down the aisle, and at my row she turned and slid in beside me.

I exhaled, then breathed in the cold morning air from her coat, from her hair as she yanked off her hat. Static snapped and glowed like lightning bugs. Our legs touched, tensed, then relaxed through the shifting gears. I cherished these soft moments before the glare, the hard-edged asceticism of second grade, Immaculate Conception Elementary School.

The poet Muriel Rukeyser wrote "Pay attention to what they tell you to forget." If love is simply paying attention, then, playing fast and loose with love's silly-gism, we must love what they tell us to forget.

Thirty years later, bouncing along on another bus, staring outside at the lightening sky and at myself in the window, I remembered those early rides, that early love, that breathless attention to every detail of her. Riding with my lover snuggled deep inside her down coat, her breath rhythmic and sweet sighing in and out of her coat, her sleeping weight on my shoulder, we drove all night back from the march, back in time for work.

We had left almost 24 hours earlier, in the

dark blue morning, layered against the cold, cups of coffee steaming, waking to each other, waiting for our bus. It materialized before our staring eyes, and we loaded in, backpacks, bail money and signs. When we arrived near the start of the march, we received our instructions and left the warm protection of the bus for the glare of hate and press.

We marched grimly, defiantly, pink triangles on green shamrocks, through gauntlets of screaming, cursing Hibernians. I witnessed one older woman, gray hair tucked in her tam, shriek so vehemently she spat out her dentures. They seemed to hang mid-air, then clatter to the street. She saw me see it and after a split second of horror, she screamed again and bent to scoop them up. We continued to the end of the parade route, dazed, slimed, but undaunted.

As we rode back through the night, I could feel the acid hate of the day eat at the sheaths of my nerves; I was too wired to sleep. I lifted my lover down from my shoulder, slid her down my chest to my lap and patted her that everything was all right. I heard my friends shifting in sleep around me, a murmured conversation, a soft giggle, a kiss. And suddenly I remembered that I had first kissed a woman long, on her lips, in her car on St. Patrick's Day, 1975, in Boston. No wonder those Hibernians were crazy. Pay attention to what they tell you to forget.

NEW YORK, NEW YORK
*Roy Strickland and William Wynkoop, members of SAGE
and a couple for forty-three years.*
PHOTOGRAPH BY C.T. WEMPLE

SEATTLE, WASHINGTON
*Morgan, eighteen, doubles Madigan, also eighteen,
on her bike. They've been out lovers since fifteen.*
PHOTOGRAPH BY DANA SCHUERHOLZ

NEW YORK, NEW YORK
Some still sleep.
PHOTOGRAPH BY GREG WEINER

NEW YORK, NEW YORK
Daji and Jevona Anderson celebrating
Gay Pride at the west side piers.
PHOTOGRAPH BY SARAH FEINSMITH

NEW YORK, NEW YORK
*William Phillips and Rodney Kiester before begin-
ning a busy day at home and office.*
PHOTOGRAPH BY KLAUS SCHOENWIESE

NORTHAMPTON, MASSACHUSETTS
*Smith College students Libby Lewis and
Nicholette Roemer, off-campus.*
PHOTOGRAPH BY MARILYN HUMPHRIES

WASHINGTON, D.C.
A cleric and his lover state their commitment at the
March on Washington gay and lesbian wedding.
PHOTOGRAPH BY CINDY REIMAN

CHICAGO, ILLINOIS
A typical Friday evening for Laura McAlpine, Ann McCallister, and Amalia.
PHOTOGRAPH BY PETER ROSS

SEATTLE, WASHINGTON
*Catherine, Angela, and Liz in the studio
apartment they share on Capitol Hill.*
PHOTOGRAPH BY DANA SCHUERHOLZ

BROOKLYN, NEW YORK
*Catching the bouquet at a lesbian
wedding ceremony.*
PHOTOGRAPH BY DONNA BINDER

NEW YORK, NEW YORK
Robert Reid and Jack McNeil register as domestic partners.
PHOTOGRAPH BY MARK PETERSON

TAMPA, FLORIDA
Lesbian Avengers en route to a political action.
PHOTOGRAPH BY CAROLINA KROON

WASHINGTON, D.C.
1993 March on Washington mass wedding.
PHOTOGRAPH BY TERRY GYDESEN

CHICAGO, ILLINOIS
Joseph Conlon and William Cordero after their commitment ceremony.
PHOTOGRAPH BY GARY HANNABARGER

NEW YORK, NEW YORK
Supportive spectators at a Gay Pride march.
PHOTOGRAPH BY CLARK JONES

LOS ANGELES, CALIFORNIA
Melissa Etheridge and her partner, Julie Cypher.
PHOTOGRAPH BY F. SCOTT SCHAFER

Fireplace

I'D NEVER SPENT A NIGHT IN THIS HOUSE, MY FATHER'S HOUSE, WITH A
BOYFRIEND. TO MAKE IT RIGHT, TO RESTORE ITS OWN CAPACITY FOR
ROMANCE, I HAD TO EXORCISE THE DUSTY SPIRITS OF DEFEAT AND OBLIGATION.

by Frank Browning

Tools were the first question.

Which tools would be necessary to break through the cemented-up brick wall covering the mouth of the fireplace? My parents had had it sealed off fifty years earlier, during the Depression, and replaced it with a fuel oil heater to warm their house for their first child. Since I was a child I'd always wanted to reopen the fireplace.

I'd imagined marvelous mysteries stashed away and covered with soot just beyond the masonry, fragments from the time when both the house and the farm were full of romance. Chips of the hollow-stemmed champagne glasses my father told me he had once thrown into the burning logs. The missing brass andirons that had been handed down from some obscure ancestor. Or maybe lost pages of poems he had written in the twenties (his twenties), when he lived in Provence with his first wife, before his romantic spirit had been broken with her death and the Depression's arrival and the stark reality of living cold winters alone in that converted log house on an isolated hilltop in eastern Kentucky.

I'd imagined lying on faded oriental rugs before the fireplace, snuggling, caressing, recalling earlier delicious evenings on the wet paving stones of the Place de la Concorde, when love was fresh and the future infinite

and apples were not just a crop, but poetry.

In just a few weeks my new boyfriend (my first real one in longer than I could remember) would arrive from New York for the holidays. My father's first wife, Betty, had come from "back East" (well, Pittsburgh, but they'd met back there, when she was a Smithie and he a Yalie). Various aunts, uncles, and cousins who'd moved East would visit or pass through during my childhood, opening up vistas of excitement, intelligence, and enchantment. (And yes, one even brought me my first original Broadway cast album.) But the house itself, a pleasant, two-story, three-bedroom building framed around a central cabin of twelve-by-twelve poplar logs, was a hazy place where the images of exotic cities were clouded in bittersweet memory and too much cigarette smoke.

Gene's arrival would be more than a confirmation of our new relationship. We'd just finished two weeks of exploratory vacation together, driving through the English countryside of Somerset, then staying with friends of mine in Paris. We'd broken all the standard advice against embarking on foreign travel too early in the affair, and we'd survived, more tolerant, more appreciative of the temperamental quirks that come with middle age. Not only was it clear we cared about each other. We enjoyed each other. His arrival for the holidays, in the place where all the childhood emotions evoked by Christmas had been born, would finally break open all the old entrapments I'd felt there as an adult gay man.

I wanted the fireplace ready by then.

I'd never spent a night in this house, my father's house, with a boyfriend. To make it right, to restore its own capacity for romance (and, I suppose, to release my own capacity for romance), I had to exorcise the dusty spir-

its of defeat and obligation that had settled into the logs, to open the firebox and let them escape up the chimney with the smoke of burning applewood. Not that I wanted to erase my father's memory from the place, or the memory of his first wife, or of my mother. Their traces are indelibly preserved in scores of household artifacts: a small blue Rookwood vase, the heavy black walnut desk, several framed pieces of brightly colored crewel stitchery. By opening the fireplace I wanted only to release the torpor that for too long had left no room for lovemaking. (Already, on a trip to Central Asia, I'd bought my own oriental carpet to cover the floor before the fireplace.)

The original hearthstones were still in place, soft, polished, gray rectangles half covered by a utilitarian wall-to-wall rug. The fireplace itself was grand—nearly five feet from one side to the other, large enough to crawl inside if you bent your knees and lowered your neck. A thin cement frosting, painted gray in the fifties, masked the opening.

I took an old clawhammer and tapped. The eight-pound sledgehammer I'd borrowed from a neighbor seemed unnecessary.

A crack formed. Then another. I slipped a wood chisel into the cracks and twisted. The tired cement came loose in great, crispy flakes, exposing an inner wall of super-hardened, yellow firebricks. A few more taps and a little more chipping against the mortar with a broken screwdriver, and the first brick fell free.

The wall to the firebox was stacked only one layer thick. Breaking through proved easier than I'd imagined. A quarter hour later a dozen more bricks had given way, forming a ruin of broken corners. I peered through the hole to see how much more work it would take before I could start bringing in new logs.

MONTICELLO, NEW YORK
Kady and Pagan clearing a path at their upstate cabin.
PHOTOGRAPH BY JEB

PROVINCETOWN, MASSACHUSETTS
*Urvashi Vaid, author and former executive director of the
National Gay and Lesbian Task Force, takes a call.*
PHOTOGRAPH BY PASCAL DE LAUBIER

Chalo beautifies a backyard.
PHOTOGRAPH BY HENNY GARFUNKEL

206

PORTLAND, OREGON
*Lovers Paul and Fred relax in their
hot tub at home.*
PHOTOGRAPH BY LINDA KLIEWER

JAMAICA PLAIN, MASSACHUSETTS
Pam and Josie share a light.
PHOTOGRAPH BY LIZ LINDER

MIAMI, FLORIDA

Robert Lewis creates wicker lamps for his company,
Haywire, in his South Beach front yard.

PHOTOGRAPH BY ALEXIS RODRIGUEZ-DUARTE

LAS VEGAS, NEVADA
Dale at Sierra Safari Zoo with Hobbs, a liger—
half tiger, half lion.
PHOTOGRAPH BY DONNA BINDER

NEW YORK, NEW YORK
*Hal Gomeau and John Harbster clear away Sunday
breakfast dishes. The couple met at SAGE and have
been together for ten years.*
PHOTOGRAPH BY TOM MCKITTERICK

NEW YORK, NEW YORK
Pianist John Corigliano prepares a score.
PHOTOGRAPH BY T.L. LITT

CHARLESTON, WEST VIRGINIA
Bob Miller and Tim Poston, owners of a bed
and breakfast, go over their monthly bills.
PHOTOGRAPH BY MITZI KELLOGG

SAN FRANCISCO, CALIFORNIA
Author Armistead Maupin and his lover,
Terry Anderson, relax in their living room.
PHOTOGRAPH BY HARUKO

San Francisco, California
Judy Grahn, poet, gardening.
PHOTOGRAPH BY PHYLLIS CHRISTOPHER

PROVINCETOWN, MASSACHUSETTS
*Bob O'Malley and associate Maryellen Gould of Beachfront
Realty, with a couple interested in buying a country home.*
PHOTOGRAPH BY PASCALE DE LAUBIER

LINCOLN, NEBRASKA
*Before heading to a day job, Sheri Overly cleans
up around her place.*
PHOTOGRAPH BY ROBIN TRIMARCHI

After presents in bed, Brenda Culver leads Cindy Chasteen into the
living room she has decorated for Cindy's twenty-eighth birthday.
PHOTOGRAPH BY LISA A. DAVIS

San Francisco, California
Jewelle Gomez, essayist and author, at her home.
PHOTOGRAPH BY PHYLLIS CHRISTOPHER

WASHINGTON, D.C.
*Home is where these hearts are, for two couples at the
1993 March on Washington.*
PHOTOGRAPHS BY BROOKS KRAFT/SYGMA

Author Biographies

MARGARETHE CAMMERMEYER was reinstated as Chief Nurse of the Washington State National Guard after being discharged from her post under a regulation banning homosexuals from serving in the military. An army nurse for nearly three decades, Colonel Cammermeyer has had a distinguished career, including receipt of a Bronze Star for service in Vietnam.

MICHAEL GOFF is editor and president of OUT magazine, which he founded in 1992.

ERIC K. WASHINGTON is the New York editor of *BLK* and has contributed to *The Village Voice, Metropolis, Transition,* and *Elle Decor.*

ROBIN STEVENS is a freelance writer and editor living in San Francisco. She is a former editor of *Outlook,* the national lesbian and gay quarterly, and is editor of the anthology *Girlfriend Number One: Lesbian Life in the '90s.*

JESS CAGLE, a senior writer for *Entertainment Weekly* magazine, came of age in Abilene, Texas, where he spent many hours in his room with his prized collection of Joan Crawford memorabilia. He attended Baylor University, near the Branch Davidian compound in Waco. He now lives in Manhattan, and is trying to forget.

ERIC MARCUS is the author of several books, including *Making History: The Struggle for Gay and Lesbian Equal Rights, 1945 to 1990.* He is also co-author of the forthcoming autobiography of Olympic diving champion Greg Louganis. Marcus has been an unenthusiastic jogger for the past thirteen years.

RENEE GRAHAM is a feature writer for *The Boston Globe.* Her work has also appeared in *African Voices, Sojourner, Nieman Reports,* and *Women's Own.* A native of Queens, New York, she lives in Brookline, Massachusetts.

CHANDLER BURR is an international journalist now based in Washington, D.C., who has written for PBS, *The Atlantic Monthly, The New York Times Magazine,* the *Christian Science Monitor,* and many other publications. His book on the biological search for the origin of sexual orientation is due to be published by Hyperion. Burr is also a playwright.

LILY ENG is a board member of National Gay and Lesbian Journalists Association and a staff reporter for *The Seattle Times.*

MICHAEL MUSTO writes "La Dolce Musto," the weekly entertainment column in *The Village Voice,* "Pop Life," a pop culture column in *Spin,* and is a regular contributor to OUT and *Vanity Fair.* Musto has authored two books, *Downtown* and *Manhattan on the Rocks.*

KATE CLINTON is a humorist. Her hobbies are tatting, garnishing, and world revolution.

FRANK BROWNING writes for National Public Radio and is the author of *Culture of Desire.*

Index of Photographers